VAIN

Selene Michaelson

VAIN

I stared down at Isabella's head in the box and I couldn't stop myself. How could they do this to her? My heart felt like it had been ripped out of my chest. I couldn't breathe and I was blinded by rage. I grabbed my gun and walked towards the door quickly. My father grabbed me before I could leave. Why was he stopping me? I was going to kill Satoni's ass, and he couldn't stop me. There was nothing that he could do to me anymore. He took away the one thing that made me happy, and now I was going to kill his sorry ass.

"I'm going to make him regret this shit."

My father pushed me down on the couch. "I know that you're angry, but you have to be smart. Keep your head in the game because if you don't you'll end up dead. He wanted blood for what you did to his sister and now he got it."

"I DIDN'T KILL HER!"

He grabbed me by the collar, "watch your tone. I told you that this lifestyle is not for women. If you decide to have a wife, remember that she will be used against you. You knew that when you started dealing with her. If you want to blame someone, blame yourself. You're the one who left her with no protection. You know that you are supposed to leave her with security."

He was right, I had fucked up. I left her unprotected and that gave them the opportunity to kidnap her. It was my fault that she was dead, but I still wanted to kill them.

"I won't let you start a war over a girl."

"She wasn't any girl; she was the love of my life. She was carrying my baby and they murdered her. Do you have any idea what I'm going through right now? I don't think you do because you have the woman that you love."

He sighed running his fingers through his hair, "you're right. I don't know what it's like, but that doesn't change the rules. If she was your wife, it would be different, but she wasn't. She was a girl that you were fucking and you caught feelings. Move on and get over it because we will get them back."

"How?" I asked tucking my gun in my waistband.

He handed me a drink and I took it. "They have a container of cocaine heading to Texas. We are going to take it; they will lose six hundred thousand."

"That sounds good," I mumbled downing my drink in one gulp.

He smirked and patted me on the shoulder, "I'm placing you in charge. Kill as many of their men as possible. That will be your revenge, and you know you only get one shot."

"I won't mess it up, I'll take advantage of this." I stood up and my mom walked into the room. I knew that she didn't like when I went on missions like this, but she had to understand that I needed to do this.

"Vain, I don't think this is a good idea."

"Mom, I'm not in the mood for a lecture right now. I need to handle this and I will. Did you see what they did to her?"

She sighed, "yeah. But you know that killing will never make things right. It won't bring her back."

"They started this war, and I'm going to finish it." I walked out of the room before she could say another word. There was no way that they were going to get away with this.

When I arrived at the location where the drop was being made, I was surprised to see Roman with his father. The Romano family had them picking it up? What the hell was going on? I sat in my car and watched as Roman and his father joked with each other. I couldn't stop the surge of jealousy that surged through me. They always had a good relationship, and I was envious of it. Roman was eighteen and he had grown to be tall just like his dad. He looked just like his father, but he had his mother's smile. They weren't even treating this like a mission as I watched them play wrestle. That was the one thing that I hated about their family. They were pure, not an ounce of evil in them. Why couldn't my family be like that? The trucks started to arrive and my men and I started to prepare to shoot, but I stopped when I noticed a girl walking towards them. She was yelling at them and I couldn't make out what she was saying. I held my hand up to hold off my men. Why was a girl here and who was she? She was wearing a pair of short denim shorts, a white crop top, and white and black Dior sneakers. Her long black hair was blowing in the wind as she made her way over to them. She was young, but she was so beautiful and her body was already very developed.

"DAD, HURRY UP!" She screamed placing her hand on her hip. "I'M HUNGRY AND YOU PROMISED ME PIZZA."

Roman jogged over to her quickly, "dad is busy. We told you to wait in the car. We will be there in a minute."

She rolled her eyes, "ugh what are you two doing anyway? I've been waiting for ten minutes."

He shoved her, "go wait in the car. Don't come back."

"You're not the boss of me," she snapped back.

Alonzo walked over to them and wrapped his arms around them. "Both of you stop it now. Athena, go wait in the car, sunshine. I promise I'm coming." She sighed loudly and turned around making her way towards the car that was a distance away.

Athena...that was Athena? I hadn't seen her since she was a baby. She was gorgeous, she had really grown into her looks. She looked just like her mom, and her smile took my breath away.

"Vain, what are you doing? We need to go ahead and get the trucks."

I turned to look at Ace and shook my head slowly. "No, the mission is off."

He stared at me confused, "what the hell? What are you talking about? Your dad is going to be pissed if we don't get these trucks."

I started the car, "I said the mission is off. Don't question me about it."

He sat back in his seat and mumbled something that I couldn't understand. I knew that if we opened fire, they would die. Even though I wanted to make Satoni suffer, I couldn't kill Alonzo. I wouldn't kill him in front of his kids. I was pissed off but I wasn't evil. Besides, my issue wasn't with the Vintalli family, it was with Satoni and his people. The Vintalli's were in the wrong place at the wrong time. But I had a feeling that Satoni did it on purpose.

My father slammed his hand down on the desk. I knew that he was going to be angry that I canceled his mission, but I didn't care. I couldn't stop thinking about Athena. Damn, she had to be about fifteen now, right? I placed my hand on my chin and thought about it. When was the last time I had seen them? Athena was about one year old, had it been that long?

"Are you listening to me?"

I raised an eyebrow, "yeah." I wasn't but I was telling him what he wanted to hear.

"Why the hell did you cancel the mission?"

"Because Alonzo was there and he had Roman with him."

He frowned, "so what? They are the enemy as well, have you forgotten that?"

I sighed, "no. But Athena was there too. I wasn't about to kill him in front of his daughter. She's only fifteen, and she didn't need to see something like that."

He stared at me for a second before laughing, "are you serious? You stopped my mission because of a little girl. Vain, where the hell is your head at right now? You aren't thinking clearly."

I leaned back in my chair and tried to keep my temper under control. "I did what I felt was the best thing to do. You said yourself that we can't go around creating unnecessary wars. They are not the enemy right now but killing them would start one. My issue is with Satoni, not with some third party that works for him."

"I gave you an order," he growled.

"I'm not about to have that kind of blood on my hands. If you want it so badly go kill him. But I want no parts of it. I'm glad that I saw her when I did because she would have been dead."

He stared at me for a second before sitting down in his chair. "I feel like it was stupid what you did, but I trust your decision and quick thinking. Alonzo isn't an enemy of ours and he is very resourceful. Besides, he still has two parts of New York. So, that means that we have to get along with him for now. I hate that Satoni did that shit though. He knew what we had planned and planned in advance. He is a smart kid; I'll give him that. His father left him in charge and showed him all the loopholes."

"He has what is coming to him, I can guarantee you that."

My father frowned, "you said that Athena was there, right?"

"Yeah, why?"

"You know that is Satoni's soon-to-be bride," he smirked.

I sat up quickly, "what? How do you know?"

"I'm a mafia leader, Alonzo told me. He said that he wanted Athena to be safe when she reached the age of eighteen. So, he decided that once Athena turns eighteen, she will be Satoni's wife."

I gripped the arm of the chair trying to calm myself down. "I never thought that he would make a decision like that."

"It makes sense. We need to make sure that the little girl doesn't go tainting any more mafia bloodlines. I think it will be best for her to be with Satoni. You know that he is tainted blood too. They can make filthy blooded babies and we can rest easy knowing she is with him. It's a win-win situation."

I shook my head, "I think it's stupid. If they get married they will have access to even more resources. That would make the Romano family even stronger and richer."

He laughed, "you don't miss a thing. But that works to our advantage. You wanted revenge and you will have your revenge."

"What do you mean?"

"Why don't you enjoy his bride before he does. Imagine if you were her first, he would never be able to change that. Making her fall in love with you is the best revenge for him. Taking something that rightfully belongs to him is the best way to get back at him."

I smiled and nodded my head slowly, "I see what you're saying."

One thing about my father was the fact that he was smart. He always wanted to destroy people from the inside out. He thought that death was too easy. He wanted to do things to people that would last them a lifetime. I thought that it was a good idea at the time, and I decided to do it. He took something from me and so I would do the same to him. I never hurt his sister, but he was too blind to see that. Now, he was going to regret taking Isabella from me. I would have gotten married and changed to be a better man for her. But now that she was gone...I was reborn.

I was a devil...and I loved it.

I hope you all enjoyed this chapter

Contents

1. Vain — 1

2. AYA — 3

3. PRICE — 9

4. PRESENT — 16

5. FILTHY BLOOD — 23

6. RUSH & ROULETTE — 30

7. RUSH & ROULETTE 2 — 37

8. ADD UP — 45

9. A DEVIL — 54

10. SEX DICE — 61

11. SEX DICE 2 — 67

12. ISABELLA — 73

13. 3RD GAME — 80

14. BASKETBALL — 86

15. SATONI — 92

16. DAY OF REST   93

17. VICTOR GREY   99

18. HEARTLESS   106

19. DREAM OR REALITY   115

20. TELL ME   122

21. CHIARA   129

22. BLACKMAIL   137

23. I LOVE YOU   143

24. SEE YOU IN HELL   150

25. EPILOGUE   162

Vain

M arch 19th 2022

This book is very explicit and mature. It contains strong adult language, mature scenes, Sex scenes and abuse. Mature audience only please .

Hello guys, I am very excited to announce this new book that will be coming out very soon. I want to start off by saying that this book is not a continuation of Athena's story. This story is about Aya and Vain and you will see characters from the previous books. But this is not a sequel to the tainted Scars series.

Book #3 (Tainted IV Series)

"Why are you doing this?" I whispered watching as he came closer.

"Because you remind me of someone."

"She must mean a lot to you." I gasped when he pinned me to the wall.

"She stole my heart and never gave it back." He smirked eyeing me up and down slowly. "Let's see if you can get away from me like she did."

Aya Varloni lives a quiet life with her brother. She doesn't know much about what he does and she knows not to question him. On her twenty first birthday she is shocked to come home to find men in her house waiting for her. One of them is sexy but she knows he is dangerous. He tells her that he is Vain Grey, a mafia leader. He tells her that her brother has gambled away a lot of his money and she is going to play a game with him. She will spend 6 months with him and she will play ten games. If she wins he will overlook her brother's debt and give her one million dollars. If she loses.. she is his for a year and her brother dies. Aya has never gambled before but now she was gambling with her life.

AYA

The gun was pointed right at his head and there was nothing I could do. The room was silent before the sound of the gun went off.

I screamed falling to my knees.

WAIT!!! I think we jumped too far ahead.

Sorry, let me start from the beginning. My name is Aya Varloni and I'm twenty-one years old. I was born on July 11th in New York City. I'm into astrology so my zodiac sign is Cancer. I am small for my age but I never complained about it. I'm 5'5 in height and I weigh about 120 pounds. I have a small curvy figure and I like it. My midnight black hair flowed down to my waist. My eyes were dark brown and I was blessed with thick lashes. I'm mixed with Italian and Korean. My father is Italian and my mother is Korean. Unfortunately, they died when I was seventeen in a fire. My father was a chef and he had his own restaurant. It was called Mino's Pizzeria. The restaurant was named after my mother Mino. My father's name was Kyle. I miss them so much every day but they didn't leave me alone. I was blessed with an older brother. Did I say blessed, I actually meant cursed. Aito was my biggest headache, and we argued about everything. We argue about the weather, who lost the remote, and who is going to take the garbage out. He is such a big-headed jerk and he loves to pick on me. I would love to say that we started to get along after our parents died but that's not true. He always uses the same sentence to manipulate me into doing things. He always says if mom and dad were still here. My brother is a total ladies' man. Aito is twenty-five years old. He is about 6 ft in height and has short black hair that's short in the back and long in the front. Trust me, the girls love him. He is covered in tattoos that he started getting when he was sixteen but he is very handsome. Despite the piercings that he has under his eye and on his lip. We both take after our mom but my dad never complained. I feel like Aito was gifted with his height because I'm short just like my mother. My brother and I live in our family home. We grew up in the house and it's the only home that I've ever known. Were lucky that mom and dad paid the house off after they died because we were able to stay here. We still had bills but at least we didn't have to worry about where we would live. I spend a lot of my time at work because the bills won't pay themselves and I'm attending college. My brother has a job but I don't question him about it. The last time that I did, he flipped out and told me to stay out of his business. So, as long as he has his half of the bills, I don't care. Just as long as it's nothing illegal because I don't have the money to bond him out of jail but knowing him, he probably did. But enough about my brother, I'm in college to be a nurse. I graduate in a year and I couldn't be happier about it. I work at a paint store helping people pick colors of paint when they are redecorating their homes or offices. It keeps me busy and I work Monday through Friday until four in the evening. As much as I loved my job, I took a vacation because today was my birthday. I decided to go shopping because I needed a new outfit. I had my whole day planned out because I was finally turning twenty-one. I had one friend and I had known her since elementary school. Her name was Kimi and she was like a sister to me.

Kimi was 5'4 in height and she had short black hair that stopped at her shoulders and light brown eyes. She was one hundred percent Korean and she was proud. She had the cutest smile and laugh. She knew everything about me and I knew everything about her. We were inseparable but I didn't mind. I was a very shy girl so it was hard for me to make new friends. I was a loner but I didn't mind. I loved being alone and cuddling up in bed with snacks and a movie after work. But Kimi told me that I needed to get a social life and she was right. I hadn't even had a boyfriend yet and that is odd. I was still a virgin but I was waiting for the right man. Kimi lost her virginity when she was fifteen and she always told me that it wasn't so bad. She wanted me to lose it so that we could gossip about it but I wasn't ready. She would tease me and tell me that I would be a forty-year-old virgin if I kept waiting. But I didn't mind at all because it was something that I cherished.

"Are you listening to me?"

I looked over and smiled, "yeah. You said that you wanted to get Ben's attention tonight. Trust me, you will. You have the sexiest dress and it's his favorite color."

She shrugged, "I hope so. By the way, there is something that I need to talk to you about. I have been keeping it to myself for a while but I know that I need to be honest with you."

I frowned and stopped walking so that I could look at her. It was strange when she kept secrets from me because she never did. She told me everything no matter how big or small. The fact that she was keeping something from me meant that it was not going to be good.

"So, I decided to take the scholarship and go to Harvard."

My mouth dropped open. Kimi and I went to college together but she wanted to be a lawyer. She was doing amazing in class and she had a 3.9 GPA. I was there when she got her letter in the mail from Harvard. She was so excited about it and I was happy too but I wasn't happy about her leaving me.

"That's great, but I thought that you said that you didn't want to go."

She sighed, "yeah. But I thought about it and I feel like I should take the opportunity. My mom is pushing me to go and they are giving me a full ride there. I'll eventually have to start coming out of pocket here at Bayside University. I love it but I have to take this opportunity that was given to me."

I crossed my arms over my chest, "I'm happy for you. Trust me, I understand and I know that you have to do what's best for you. But I'm not jumping for joy for you to leave. You are my best friend and now I'm losing you."

She pulled me into a hug, "you're not losing me. Listen, Harvard is four hours away from us."

"It's in Massachusetts," I mumbled.

She laughed, "which is about four hours away. I'll come to visit every weekend."

I rolled my eyes, "don't lie to me. You'll be too busy studying to come to visit every weekend."

"You're not making this easy on me, Aya."

I ran my fingers through my hair, "I can say the same for you. I thought that we said that we would finish college here. We made plans for the summer and now you're just up and leaving."

"I know but there is no way that we will finish together. You are going to be a nurse and you finish in a year. I'm going to be a lawyer and I have five more years to go. At least I'll be surrounded by people who understand and go through what I do. Harvard is the school for lawyers, Aya."

I stared down at my feet, "do what makes you happy."

She grabbed my hand, "it's just a part of growing up. I'm not doing this because I want to leave you behind. But I know that for me to be successful, I have to work hard. I'll call you every night and...look, it won't be the same. I'm not going to sit here and lie to you but we have to make the best of it."

"I know and I agree with you but I hate that you told me on my birthday. It's like my day is ruined now."

"No, we are going to have fun. We have to have fun because I'm leaving tomorrow."

My eyes widened, "tomorrow? Wow, that's just great. You know what, I don't want to talk about it anymore." I turned to walk away and she grabbed me.

"Aya, stop being so stubborn."

"I'm being stubborn? You're my best friend, Kimi. You are my sister and I feel like I'm losing you. You tell me on my birthday that you're leaving tomorrow. Who am I going to have coffee dates with? Who am I going to shop with? I'm looking at the reality of this situation. We can't have any more lunch dates. How will I get through work without you being there to help me laugh? You don't understand how everything is changing now."

"You don't think I feel the same way, huh? You think I'm skipping away into the sunset? It's hurting me to leave you, Aya. I will have no one when I go to Harvard. I'll be the new girl and I'll be doing the same thing. I'll have lunch by myself, coffee, shopping, and being alone at work. I wish that I could take you with me but I can't. You have a life here and you have to finish your degree. It's just a part of growing up, Aya. You have to learn that in life stuff like this is going to happen. We are going to get married, have kids, and relocate. I love New York and I'm leaving the only home that I know. But It's only temporary because once I get my degree, I'm coming home. Trust me, I will still make time to come to see you, and we can still have the summer we planned."

I wiped away my tears and pulled her into a hug. She was right, she was going to be alone just like me. Instead of being stubborn, I needed to be there for her when she needed me the most.

"I'm going to Harvard, not prison."

I laughed and pulled away. She wiped away her tears and smiled at me. "I'm sorry, I should have been more supportive of you."

"It's okay, I'm used to your stubborn ways. Now, let's finish shopping so that we can party."

She grabbed my hand and pulled me into another store. I was happy that we got to talk about it but it still hurt me that she was leaving. Now that she was fulfilling her dreams, I knew that I had to do the same thing. I wanted to be just as successful as she was and I knew that meant that I had to work harder. I wanted to make her proud and so I decided to turn my sadness into determination. I was going to graduate from Bayside so that I could keep that memory alive and I knew that she would do the same thing. She was the type of friend that would dedicate her success to people she cared about. I wanted her to be the best lawyer that she could be and I would be right beside her, no matter where it took her. I didn't understand it when they said that after high school it would only get harder. Now, I knew why they said that.

I hope you all enjoyed this chapter

PRICE

V AIN

It's been a while since I confronted someone about debt but this couldn't be ignored. Ace hired this guy to help us flip money and he was doing a good job. But that slowly started to go downhill and instead of helping us, he decided to play with my money. I had my eyes on him for weeks thinking that maybe he would get himself together but he kept going downhill. So, now it was time to confront him and kill him. I didn't have time for people who decided to play instead of work. It was annoying and I didn't want anyone like that on my team. I walked into the room and sighed rolling up my sleeves. Ace was in the room with another one of my men. There was a guy tied to a chair in the middle of the room. He was covered in tattoos and he looked Asian. I sat in the chair in front of him and I could see the fear in his eyes. But there was something else that I noticed. He was afraid but he had a fighting spirit, I could tell. Instead of putting a bullet in his head, I decided to take it easy on him for a minute.

"What's your name kid?"

"Aito," he said. His voice held dominance but was gentle at the same time.

"Cool name, I like it. As much as I would like to sit here and get to know you on a friendship level, I can't. You see, you have gambled away five hundred thousand dollars of my money. Ace warned you two months ago and I still see no progress with you recovering the money you lost. What the hell is going on? Do you think this is a game?" He gulped and I smirked. I could see it now, the fear in his eyes.

"Listen, I would never play with your money. I do different things to flip your money and gambling is one of them."

I pulled my gun out and pointed it at him. "Don't lie to me, Aito. I'm not in the mood to listen to your bullshit. Don't beat around the bush with me. Just come and say the truth because either way, you're dead."

Ace stepped in front of me, "I know you're upset but listen to me. This kid is good at what he does."

"He can be replaced," I mumbled.

Ace laughed, "I don't think you're going to find someone who can bring in half a million every month. Let's be honest here, he had brought in five times the amount of money that he lost. Trust me, I get it. You don't want people getting over on you but this kid is special. He is a big part of the family and the business that he runs. Hear him out and then decide what you want to do. But don 't kill him, Vain. I want you to trust me on this one. He's smart as hell and I've never seen anyone like him."

He stepped aside and I sighed sticking my gun back on my waist. Usually, Ace wanted to kill, but I knew that if he was vouching for him, he had to be good at what he did.

"You want the truth; I'll give it you."

I raised an eyebrow and smirked. Ace was right, this kid had spirit and I liked it.

"I've been flipping money for you and Ace is right. I have made a lot of money doing it the way that I'm used to. I thought that maybe if I went to the Casino, I could flip money there. It was risky but I knew the money that they have there. So, I decided to start off by playing with one hundred thousand. I won double the money and started to play again. It was more fun for me than it was work. I'll admit it because I can't lie to you. I stopped focusing on work and started playing for fun. One night, I had too many drinks and my head wasn't where it needed to be. I lost the five hundred thousand in one night. I've been trying to get it back ever since. It wasn't that I was ignoring your attempts to reach me. I knew that money was what you wanted and you didn't care about my excuses. So, I've been winning your money back and stacking it. I wanted to give you the whole amount at one time."

I sat back in my chair and thought about what he said. It sounded good but was it really the truth? Would he lie to me even though I told him not to? I stared at him for a second before sighing loudly. I could see his confidence and I didn't have the feeling that he was lying to me. But I still didn't know what I should do with him. He still needed to be taught a lesson, I couldn't let hi off free. He would do it again and then other people would try to get over on me. I had to make a statement and Ace knew that. Even if I didn't decide to kill him, what would his punishment be? Just as I was about to respond my assistant walked in. She handed me a folder and I thanked her in Italian. I hadn't met Aito before and so I wanted to get as much information on him as I could. This was the best way to see what he had and where he came from. I opened the folder and smirked looking down at the picture of him.

"Aito Varloni, you are twenty-five years old and you were born on September 5th in New York. You graduated from Bayside high school with a 3.9 GPA. So, you are a smart boy," I laughed. "You played Basketball and you were pretty good at it too. Oh, you're mixed with Italian and Korean.

That's an interesting mix. It says here that your parent's names are Mino and Kyle. So, which one of your parents is Italian?"

"My father," he said staring down at his feet.

I looked through his file again. "It seems that your parents died a few years ago in a car crash...that's unfortunate. So, that means that you are all alone." I looked up and he I licked his bloody lip. There was no mistaking it now, he was scared. I turned the page and looked down to see a picture of a girl in a school uniform. She was smiling holding to Aito's arm tightly. "Who is this?" I whispered running my thumb over her face. I was mesmerized by her because she looked similar to Athena. She was perfect and I couldn't hide my excitement and desire. I looked up slowly and it was clear that he wanted to lie to me.

"Who is she?"

"She's um...she is my sister."

"Is she the baby or is it you?" I leaned closer to him.

"I'm the oldest," he whispered.

"Ahh...so you are supposed to be her protector?"

As soon as I said that he nearly jumped out his chair. He struggled against the restraints but he couldn't get himself free. This was the reaction that I wanted and now I had something that he cared about.

"Please, she doesn't know about any of this. She doesn't need to be dragged into my bullshit. Just leave her alone, Vain."

I chuckled, calm down, Aito. I promise, I won't hurt her." I turned the page in the file and smiled down at her information.

"Aya Varloni, she was born July 11th in New York. Today is her birthday... well...well...happy birthday, Amore." I smirked staring down at her picture. "She graduated from Bayside High school with a 3.6 GPA. Not bad, not bad at all. If I'm correct, she might be just as smart as you. She could be very valuable to me and my business and I need someone just as smart as you on my team."

I knew that he was going to decline the offer but I didn't care. I wanted to punish him and this was the way that I was going to do it.

"Vain, I'll get you back triple the money. Please, leave my sister out of this. She is in college and she is trying to become a nurse. I don't want to take her future away."

"You know in this life that nothing is off limits when you cross me. Your own mother, girlfriend, or child could be used to collect debt. You knew that when you started working for us a year ago. I'll keep it simple for you, Aito. I promise, I will not harm your sister and no harm will come to her. You know that I'm a man of my word. So, this is how we are going to settle this. You decided to play with my money and so now I'm going to play with your life. Your sister will play some games with me. If she wins, I will give her one million dollars, I'll get her into an amazing college, and you're life and debt are cleared. Now, I'm offering you way more than I'm getting in return but I think this will be fun."

He stared at me in disgust, "what happens if she loses?"

I shrugged and closed the folder, "that's easy. You die and she is mine for a year. In that year, I can do whatever I want to her, when I want, and there is nothing she can do about it."

I knew that his back was against the wall. He couldn't tell me no and he didn't seem confident in his sister.

"What type of games will you be playing?"

I was glad that he was asking questions because it made me more excited. "Gambling games. Think of it like this, you gambled with my money and now I'm going to gamble with your life. Let's see if luck is on your side, my friend."

I stood up and turned to leave the room. I was ready to get my opponent so that we could go over the rules.

"Where are you going?" He growled once again struggling against the ropes that held him to the chair.

"I'm going to go give the birthday girl her present. I'll make sure that she knows that it is a gift from her big brother Aito." I turned away from him but stopped when he called my name.

"Vain, don't hurt her, I swear."

"I won't hurt her," I cut him off before he could continue. "I have no reason to hurt her, Aito. As long as she does everything that I tell her to, she will be fine. I'm sure once she knows that your life is on the line, she will gladly submit to me. Unless there is something about her that I don't know. You can tell me now so that I can spare her later."

He sighed in defeat. "Aya can be very stubborn. But like you said, she will help me. She won't agree to your terms until she talks to me first. So, just have her facetime me for five minutes. She's not street smart at all. So, playing gambling games with her is going to be an easy win for you. She's smart and she catches on fast but you have to go over the rules with her. She needs to understand fully how to play. She's a sweet girl and she doesn't deserve this, so just be patient with her. I know that she will be afraid."

Hearing all of this made me even more eager to meet Aya. I knew that she was going to be fun to play with. She was stubborn and I loved them like this. I couldn't help but wonder if she was feisty. If she was, she would be just like Athena for sure. I told him that I understood and left the room quickly.

"Sto venendo per te...Amore." (I'm coming for you)

I hope you all enjoyed this chapter

PRESENT

I had an amazing birthday dinner with Kimi and now it was time to get home. I knew that Aito was going to be in his own world but I wanted to at least see him for my birthday. I brought him home a steak with a loaded baked potato for dinner, and I knew that he would enjoy it. I smiled and pulled my key out of my pocket quickly.

Kimi honked the horn, and I turned around and waved one more time before she drove off. I was supposed to be meeting her tomorrow afternoon to send her off to Harvard. It was still so hard watching her leave but I enjoyed my birthday with her. She made my day special and that's all that I could have asked for. I pushed the key into the lock and turned it until it clicked softly. I pushed the door open and stepped inside closing the door behind me. It was dark in the house but that wasn't abnormal. Aito was probably in his room watching tv or something. I turned around and locked the door before setting the plates on the table near the door.

"AITO, I'M HOME," I yelled searching for the light switch. There was no response from him and I sighed loudly. "Aito, I brought you some dinner."

I knew that if I mentioned food, he would come running. I switched on the light and slid my heels off. It was strange that he wasn't answering because it wasn't like him. I looked up and gasped loudly when I saw three men in my living room. One man was sitting on my couch and he had a man standing on each side of him. My mind was going crazy and I didn't know what to do. Were they here for Aito? Were they here to rob us? No, they would have taken what they wanted by now. Besides, the expensive-looking clothes they had on told me enough. They didn't need to rob us.

"Aya, right?"

I was frozen in place when he said my name. How did he know who I was? The man that was sitting on the couch smirked at me. He was handsome, no...he was sexy as hell. Everything about him screamed danger but I couldn't look away. He sat there and stared at me, his steel-grey eyes sparkling with excitement. He looked to be about just as tall as Aito from what I could see. He had broad shoulders and muscular arms that were covered in tattoos. His long eyelashes and thick eyebrows instantly made me jealous. He had high cheekbones and a jaw that could cut through steel. His dark brown hair was neat and gelled back. It was sleek and precise as if he never had a bad hair day. I had never seen a man like this before and it scared me. My heart was hammering against my chest hard. I was sure that they heard it in the quiet room.

"Who...who are you?" I whispered taking a step back.

He smirked and licked his lips. "I'm here to give you your birthday gift from Aito."

He sounded even sexier than he looked. His voice was deep and held authority. It was a mix of Italian and Spanish which fascinated me. But, I didn't like the idea of sitting down and talking to him. What the hell was he talking about? I eyed him suspiciously and he chuckled.

"Sit down and we can talk. I think that would be a good idea, don't you agree?"

I was skeptical of him but I knew that I had no chance. The only thing that I could do was listen to him even though I wanted answers now. I wanted to know where my brother was and why they were here. Did they hurt my brother? I hesitated for a minute but eventually took a seat in the armchair by the door.

"Who are you and what do you want? Where is my brother and why are you here? Did you hurt him?" I couldn't stop the questions from flying out of my mouth.

He held up his hand to silence me, "you're eager...I like it. Let's make it simple, okay? My name is Vain and your brother works for me so I'm his boss. I'm here because he gambled away my money."

I frowned, "how much money? I can pay it back." I knew that Aito was doing something that he didn't have any business doing. I knew one day that it would come to this and I hated it.

"Five hundred thousand."

My mouth flew open and I clutched my stomach. I felt sick to my stomach instantly. How the hell did he manage to do that? What the hell was he thinking? Just by looking at this man, I could tell he was a man to be feared. Why would Aito do something like this? This is why he didn't want me asking questions about what he did for a living. I cursed under my breath and closed my eyes. It would take me forever to pay him back that much money. How the hell was I going to get Aito out of trouble now?

"I will pay you back every single penny that he owes you."

He raised an eyebrow, "how do you plan to do that?"

"I don't have all the money right now but I can pay you monthly. It will take me a little bit of time but I'll get you all your money back."

"I don't think I want to wait around for you to pay me back. If you don't have all of it then we have nothing to talk about. I'm not a credit card and you won't treat me like one. Besides, your brother and I have already come up with a way to clear his debt. Do you want to know what that is?"

I nodded my head slowly. I didn't want to know but I knew that I needed to know. There was no telling what he would do to my brother and I needed to make sure that Aito stayed safe.

"Your brother decided to gamble away my money and so I decided that I would gamble with his life."

When he said that, I covered my mouth quickly. My brother was the only close family that I had left and I knew that I couldn't survive losing him. I knew that Vain wanted something and I just had to figure out what it was. He wouldn't have come to my house if he didn't want something. "What do you want? If you don't want me to pay you back then tell me what you want."

He smiled, "you are going to play some games with me. If you win, I'll let your brother go free, you get $1 million, and I will get you into any college of your choice."

All of it sounded amazing. Not only would my brother be spared but he would give me $1 million and he would get me into the college of my choice. Who was this guy and how did he have so much money and power? As much as I wanted to focus on that I couldn't because I needed to know what would happen if I lost. Most of all, I needed to know what games we were going to play and what I had to do to win.

"What happens if I lose?"

"Well, that's easy, Aya. If you lose, your brother dies and you'll be mine for a year. In that year I can do whatever I want to you and there's nothing you can do about it. Think of it like this, you'll be mine."

I gripped the arm of the chair and sat back slowly. As sexy as he was, I didn't want to spend a year with him. If I lost, my brother would die and I wouldn't let that happen. If he wanted me to play some games with him then I would.

"What games will we be playing?" I was hoping that the games would be simple.

"We are going to gamble. So, we will be playing card games, dice, and making bets. Your brother told me that you're not really good at games like that but I'll be more than happy to teach you. Now, I think that we need to discuss the rules first."

I stared at him waiting for him to break down the rules of this game. I was nervous but I couldn't let that stop me from catching every last detail of what he had to say.

"Rule number one, don't ask any questions. Rule number two, if I tell you to do something I want you to do it. Rule number three, no cheating. If I feel like you're cheating in any way, you'll lose automatically. Rule number four, Stay out of my way while you're in my home. If I take you on a business trip with me, you stay in your room."

I was confused about the last rule because I wasn't expecting to leave my house. I had a job and I couldn't just up and leave.

"That's not going to work for me. I can't just up and leave with you. I have a job and responsibilities here. I thought that I would be playing a game with you so why do I have to leave with you?"

He stood up slowly and took a step towards me. "Did you think it would be that simple? I want you to understand the reality of your situation. Your brother lost $500,000 of my money and you think one game will suffice? You couldn't be more wrong, Aya. You are going to play ten games with me. So, that means that you will spend three months with me."

He was insane and there was no way that I was going to leave with him. I stood up quickly and tried to make a run for it but he predicted my move and stopped me. He had me pinned against the door before I could even open it. I could feel his breath on my neck as he made his way up to whisper in my ear.

"You're not going to escape me that easy, Amore."

I couldn't stop my body from shaking. Warm tears slid down my cheeks before I realized I was crying. I was scared, I don't even think that was the word to describe how I felt. I didn't know what to do when I felt like my back was against the wall. If I lost these games or denied him in any way my brother would die. But at the same time, my brother was the one who got himself into the situation in the first place. None of it made sense why was it all happening on my birthday?

"Why don't you just kill us both and get it over with?" I could tell that he was a man that could end our lives and not think twice about it. He was heartless so why was he trying to give us a second chance?

"I'm used to killing but I think you got me when I'm in a better mood. Now, You need to go upstairs and grab only what you need. I'll be downstairs waiting for you."

"But I can't leave tonight. My friend is leaving tomorrow and I have to see her before she goes away. Is there any way that we can stay at least until I say goodbye to her?" I didn't want to leave without saying goodbye to Kimi but I knew that I was at his mercy.

"No, I'm a very busy man. I've already wasted enough time being here so hurry up. You have ten minutes and if you're not back downstairs in the next ten minutes, I'll come up there and get you myself."

I nodded my head slowly and tried to step past him but he stopped me. He grabbed a fistful of my hair and inhaled it deeply. "I want to speak to my brother. I won't follow any of your rules until I talk to him."

He pulled out his phone and pressed a button. The phone rang twice before Aito's face appeared on the screen.

"Oh my God, are you okay? What the hell is going on?"

He sighed, "I got myself into some deep shit. Listen to me, I need you to play those games with him. Do what he tells you to do and make sure that you pay attention so that you could win. This is not a game, Aya. I'm sorry that I got you into the situation. I know that all this is going down on your birthday and I hate it. So, I want to say happy birthday and I love you. It's going to be a while before you talk to me again but just know that I'm okay. You just focus on what needs to be done and we will see each other very soon."

Vain ended the call before I could even respond. I was glad that I got to talk to my brother and I was happy to know that he was okay. That gave me hope and it made me more determined to win. I didn't have to stay with this man forever but if I lost I would be with him a lot longer than I wanted to be. So, the only thing on my mind was winning.

I hope you all enjoyed this chapter

FILTHY BLOOD

V AIN

It was weird having Aya here with me. This was the house that Athena and I shared after we got married. I laughed and took a sip of my drink. That was the closest thing that I would ever have to a wife. I wanted to move and get another house but I didn't want to leave the memories. I stared at Aya as she slept. She reminded me so much of Athena but she wasn't feisty at all. She was shy and scared like a little kitten. But I couldn't take my eyes off her while she lay there snoring lightly. Her long black hair was scattered across the pillow and her chest rose and fell slowly. I closed my eyes and leaned back in the chair. What the hell was I doing here? Why was I watching her like this? I hated that ever since I met Athena, I couldn't get her out of my head. I dreamed of her and I only desired women who looked like her. I lifted my glass to my lips and downed the alcohol in one gulp. I loved Athena but I hated her at the same time. She came into my life and made me feel things that I never thought I would feel. But she broke my heart at the same time. Was it love? Was that the feeling that she gave me? I smirked; I wasn't capable of that. It was her virginity, that had to be it. I stood up and walked over to Aya. As I stood over her, she didn't move an inch. She was beautiful but not nearly as beautiful as Athena. We were too different and because of that, we couldn't be together. If her father hadn't married her mother, she wouldn't be tainted.

"Filthy blood," I mumbled brushing my thumb across her bottom lip. It was true, Aya was just like Athena. "He had to marry that filthy blooded Korean woman," I growled.

I closed my eyes and took a deep breath. I was losing control again and I didn't want that to happen. It was late and I needed to get some rest, so I left her room quickly. As I made my way to my bedroom, I couldn't stop thinking about what my life would have been like with Athena here. But then there was another part of me that hated her. I hated to think about her and I reminded myself every day how much of a slut she was. I pushed my room door open and walked over to my bed. I climbed in and stared at the ceiling.

"She is nothing more than filthy blood," I mumbled closing my eyes. But deep down I knew that Athena and I would be together forever and always. I had a piece of her that she would never get back. With that thought in mind, I drifted off to sleep.

I saw Roman sitting across the table from his dad. He looked scared but he was happy to be with his dad. He was six years old and I was seven. I could tell that he wasn't used to this life and I knew that I could help him. His father asked him to step out into the hallway and I decided to go with him. When we walked outside, he walked over to a car seat and smiled. I was confused at first but then I saw him lift a tiny hand. I walked over to him and quickly introduced myself.

"Hey, my name is Vain...Vain Grey."

He turned around and smiled at me nervously, "I'm Roman."

"You don't come to these often do you?"

He shook his head, "no. My father says that it's related to work but we are going to have dinner after this so we decided to tag along."

I raised an eyebrow, "who is we?"

"Oh, this is my sister Athena. She is seven months old and my mom is here too." He reached into the car seat and started to unbuckle it. After a few seconds, he pulled out a baby. She was chunky with the cutest smile and she had curly black hair.

"She's cute," I laughed waving.

"Do you have any siblings," he asked trying to hold her up. He seemed like he was struggling but he didn't drop her.

"No, it's just me, my dad, and my mom. Maybe we can hang out sometime. I like playing basketball."

He smiled, "I play football but I enjoy basketball just as much. So, I would like to play with you. I'm free on the weekends because I have school throughout the week. My mom never fails to remind me that it's a school night."

"So, you go to school?"

He frowned, "don't you?"

I shook my head, "no. I used to but my mom pulled me out. We just moved here from Spain and I didn't know English well enough to go to school here. So, I'm homeschooled."

"That seems awesome. I wish that my mom would home school me."

"ROMAN AIZEN VINTALLI, WHAT ARE YOU DOING?"

We both looked up to see a beautiful woman walking towards us. She had long black hair that flowed down her back. She was beyond beautiful; she was like an angel. She was wearing a long pink dress with matching sandals. I frowned when I noticed that she was Asian. It was forbidden to taint the mafia bloodline so who was she?

"Sorry mom, I was showing Athena to my new friend."

She scooped the baby into her arms and hugged her close. She turned around and smiled at me before turning back to face her son. "I think that was very nice of you but you have to be careful." She turned to face me again slowly, "It's very nice to meet you. What's your name?"

I shook her hand, "I'm Vain."

She giggled, "well, you are a handsome young man. I see that you take after your father."

Roman jumped in front of her, "hey mom, can we go play?"

She looked down at her watch, "um...sure but don't go too far. We will be leaving soon."

We didn't wait for a second longer after she said that. We took off running towards the doors that would lead us outside. I could hear her yelling for us to slow down and be careful but we were too excited to stop. There was a basketball court behind the building and we ran right towards it. I hadn't felt a rush like this in a long time. It had been a while since I had someone to play with. My father always reminded me of the importance of studying. He wanted me to know everything there was to know about the Mafia. I didn't have time to make friends and play outside like a normal kid. But today, I was getting a taste of what I missed so much back in Spain. He grabbed the basketball and started to dribble it across the court. He was skilled but I knew that I was better. I ran after him as he took a shot and of course, he missed. He pouted and I laughed running after the ball.

After about thirty minutes of playing, we were sweating. It was a hot summer day and the sun was shining down on us. We decided to seek shelter under a tree nearby and it turned out to be a great idea. As we lay there staring up at the clouds, a small breeze flowed past. We both laughed and closed our eyes enjoying it while it lasted. I decided to ask him the question that had been on my mind since I saw his mother.

"Your mom is Asian," I frowned.

He looked at me and smiled. "Well, she is Korean but yeah...I guess you can say that she is Asian."

"That's interesting."

He sat up slowly, "why? Is your mother Italian?"

"Yes, I'm not mixed with anything. But I think it's cool that you are. How do you handle the differences between your parents?"

He placed his hand on his lip, "well...my father has his culture and my mother has hers. But it mixes perfectly because the food is amazing. My mom is always cooking things that she ate when she was a kid. You should come over one day soon and try her famous Hana Hana noodles. Ohhh, just thinking about it is making me hungry."

His stomach growled loudly and we both burst out laughing. "I would love to try your mother's cooking."

"ROMAN, IT'S TIME TO GO!" He sat up quickly and smiled. His dad was standing next to his mom waving him over. He stood up and took off running towards them. I sat there and watched as his father picked him up and hugged him. I felt jealous watching him with his dad. My father barely hugged me and I never smiled the way Roman did.

"VAIN, COME HERE!" I looked up to see Roman calling me over. I laughed and stood up walking over to them. Roman was bouncing up and down and telling them about how we played.

"It seems like you two had a lot of fun," his dad smiled winking at me.

"Yeah, I invited him over so that he could try some of mom's Hana Hana noodles. Can he come over sometime this week?"

His mother giggled, "sure. I think it would be nice to have company."

I turned around when I heard my father calling me. He sounded irritated that I had run off and he had to go looking for me. He forced a smile when he saw me standing next to Roman. I knew that he wasn't going to be happy but maybe he would reconsider. He knew how nice this family was and they were Italian just like us.

"Dad, Roman invited me over for dinner sometime this week. Can I go?"

He sighed and stuck his hands in his pockets. "I can't make any promises because you know I have a business trip coming up. So, I'll have to get back to you on that." I felt a little sad that I wasn't going to be able to go spend more time with Roman but I knew what my father was going to say.

"Well, we have a dinner to get to, so we will see you later." His dad smiled shaking my father's hand.

Roman smiled at me, "it was fun hanging with you today. I can't wait to beat you in basketball again soon."

"You're on," I smirked.

They turned around and walked towards their car. I couldn't help but start to feel lonely watching them leave. It was an amazing day and I had fun but I didn't want it to end. A part of me wished that I could be leaving with them but I knew that my father would never let that happen. My father placed his hand on my shoulder and pulled me close.

"I don't want you playing with that boy again. They are tainted blood."

I looked up at him and frowned, "what do you mean? What does that mean?"

He kneeled in front of me slowly, "it means filthy blood. They are not fully Italian and if you ask me, they have no business being within the four families. He married that foreigner and tainted their bloodline. I can't believe it, but that's what he wanted. We don't associate ourselves with them unless we have to. Now, let's get you home so that you can get cleaned up."

It broke my heart to know that Roman and I couldn't be friends. None of it made sense, but I knew that my father took the family seriously. He didn't want us doing anything that would tarnish our name. So, I decided that I would not fight him on this and I didn't. I didn't even disagree with him when he said that Roman was going to be my biggest enemy one day.

I hope you all enjoyed this chapter

RUSH & ROULETTE

I took a shower and now I was headed downstairs to meet Vain. His house was big and beautiful. He had the prettiest décor and paintings in his home. It was two stories high but had many rooms. I felt like his house was a big museum. I walked down the stairs and into the kitchen slowly. It was just as nice as the rest of the house.

He was standing by the fridge eating a muffin and he wasn't wearing a shirt. I took a seat at the kitchen island and tried not to stare at him. Now that he wasn't wearing a shirt, I could see his tattoos clearly. I studied them as though I was studying an ancient scroll. I wondered what they meant and why he got them. My eyes stopped on a tattoo on his chest. It was the letter A with the letter V right behind it. There was a sunflower surrounding the two letters and it looked elegant. Those were my initials.

"Do you see something you like?"

I shook my head, "um...good morning." That was the only thing that I could think of. I stared down at the bowl of fruit in front of me and smiled. I loved eating fruit in the morning. It was energizing and refreshing.

"Good morning, we need to start our game today. So, we are going to play ten games in three months. The games will vary, and so will the rules. I don't like rules so there will not be that many. I'll start with the first game. We will be playing rush and roulette. I will explain more about the game once we make it to our destination."

"Okay."

"Now, in order for you to win, you have to win six of the games. If you win five and I win five, it will be a tie. We will have to do something to break the tie. Each game will last three days. So that means that whatever the game is, we will continue to play it for three days throughout the week. Whoever has the most points at the end of the week wins that game. I wouldn't mind playing all week but I'm a very busy man. Do you understand?"

I nodded my head quickly, "I understand."

"Good, now get dressed because we leave in thirty minutes." I stood up to leave, but he stepped in front of me.

"Why are you doing this?" I whispered watching as he came closer.

"Because you remind me of someone."

"She must mean a lot to you." I gasped as he pinned me to the wall.

"She stole my heart and never gave it back." He smirked eyeing me up and down slowly. "Let's see if you can escape me like she did."

He walked away leaving me standing there alone. I was happy that he wasn't trying that he was leaving things about business. But I knew that if I lost the set of games, it wouldn't be anymore. I grabbed my bowl of fruit and headed towards the stairs. I didn't want to keep him waiting.

I looked around the underground cellar and frowned. What were we doing here? Vain said that our game would start here but I didn't know why. I was grateful that there was a large window so that sunlight could pour into the room. I crossed my arms over my chest and sighed. He said that he would be back, but that was ten minutes ago. I didn't like it here and I was ready to go. Where the hell was he?

"Sei sexy oggi." (You look sexy today)

I gasped and turned around quickly. He was standing behind me smiling. I gulped and placed my hand on my heart. "You scared me," I whispered.

"Mi temi?" (Do you fear me?) He chuckled.

"I don't understand," I took a step back when he stepped towards me. He had this look in his eyes that made me uncomfortable. "Vain, what are you doing?" I continued to back away until my back hit the wall. He caged me in instantly and I could only stand there frozen in place.

"Dove stai andando?" (Where are you going?) He whispered, slipping his hand under my dress.

I pushed against his chest, "no." I didn't know what he was saying, but I knew it couldn't be good. His hand kept inching closer to my panties, and I started to panic. "Please," I whispered when he slipped his hand inside. I had never been touched by a man before. His hand felt like a foreign object to me and I didn't like it.

He chuckled, "you don't like to be touched?"

Now he was talking in English again. He was teasing me, and I didn't like it. His fingers brushed against my clit and I choked out a moan. I wanted to tell him that I was a virgin, but I didn't at the same time. What if he tried to take it from me? I closed my eyes and tried my best to endure it so that he didn't suspect anything. But when I felt his fingers trying to push inside me, I grabbed his hand.

"Please, I want you to stop."

He frowned and leaned closer, "why? Give me one good reason why I should stop?"

I gulped, "because...because I'm a virgin."

He pulled his hand away from me as if I had just burned him. He stared at me for a minute before turning his back to me. "Are you ready to hear the rules of the game?"

I was shocked at how quickly he was able to switch into a different man. I fixed my dress and told him yes. He walked over to the window and stared out, and I stood there confused. Wasn't he supposed to be telling me the rules of the game? I was about to ask him what he was doing, but I froze when three men walked into the room. One was walking towards Vain and the other two were dragging a man towards a chair. The man that they had in their arms was beaten badly. He was tied up and gagged, the sight of him caused my stomach to turn. I looked at Vain and he was staring at me smiling. What the hell did he have planned?

"Russian roulette, do you know how to play?"

I shook my head quickly, "no."

He laughed, "This will be fun. So, this game is a potentially lethal game of chance in which a player places a single round in a revolver, spins the cylinder, places the muzzle against the head or body, and pulls the trigger. If the loaded chamber aligns with the barrel, the weapon will fire, killing or severely injuring the player."

I stepped away from him quickly. Was he going to shoot me?

He smirked, "Aya, I won't hurt you. I promised your brother, and I am a man of my word. Today, this is going to be our player." He looked over at the man that was tied to the chair. "This lucky man has a chance to live or die and it depends on you and me." He was handed a gun and he walked it over to me.

I stepped away from him. He had lost his mind if he thought that I was going to play this sick game with him. I knew that I was making him angry by disobeying him, but I didn't care. He grabbed my wrist and yanked me towards his body. "Either you play or your brother dies." He pressed the gun into my hand and I trembled.

"Vain, please."

"This is how this game is going to go." He cut me off before I could say another word. There is a bullet in the gun already. There are six bullet chambers in this gun. That means that you have four chances to win and so do I. Whoever has the most points when the gun goes off wins this round. Now, we will bet on body parts, and we will bet if the gun will go off or not."

I couldn't stop the tears from sliding down my cheeks. "I don't under-stand," I whispered.

He yanked the gun away from me and walked over to the guy. "This is how it will work." He pointed the gun at the guy's foot. "You will answer, bullet or empty. Bullet means that he will be shot, and empty means, the chamber is empty. Do you understand?"

"Yes," I sobbed trying to control myself. "Empty." I didn't want to be wrong but I knew that it would be best to start off with empty. The chance of him getting shot the first time was low. Vain pulled the trigger and the gun clicked.

"You were right, luck was on your side." He walked over to me and handed me the gun. "You have to choose another body part. You can't shoot his left foot because it has already been spared.

I walked over to the guy and pointed the gun at his right foot. I didn't want to kill him, but I didn't want to hurt him either.

"Empty," Vain laughed.

I pulled the trigger and the gun clicked. I was relieved by that but I knew that the bullet was in there. I didn't know if it would fire on my turn or his. It was hard to decide now because he had a turn and so did I. He said there were six rounds in the gun. So that meant that we already used two and there were four left. I handed him the gun and he walked over to the guy quickly. He pressed the gun on his chest and my eyes widened. What was I supposed to choose? I had no idea and I didn't want to be wrong.

"Um..." Damn, this was harder than it seemed. Should I guess bullet just to be on the safe side? "Bullet."

He winked at me before pulling the trigger. The gun clicked, and I covered my mouth. I was relieved that he wasn't dead, but I knew that me being wrong earned Vain a point. He walked over to me and handed me the gun. I took it and walked over to the guy slowly. I wanted to get this over with. I hated this so much, and he knew that. I placed the gun on his thigh and stared at Vain.

"Hmmm...decisions...decisions. What should I choose? Bullet."

I pulled the trigger and the gun clicked again. I closed my eyes and sighed in relief. Now we both had two points each. I needed two more to win and so did he. I had to make sure that I was thinking this through. I walked over to him and handed him the gun. He took it from me and walked back over to him. He placed the gun on his lap and I gasped. He was making this harder and harder for me. We were down to our last two chambers and it was a fifty-fifty percent chance now. I could feel my palms sweating as I tried to make a decision.

"Empty." It had to be empty. It was empty every time we had a turn.

He cocked his head to the side, "interesting choice."

He pulled the trigger and it fired with a loud bang. I covered my mouth quickly and screamed. I could hear the man screaming, and I hated it. I covered my ears trying to unsee what I had just seen.

He walked over to me and pulled me to my feet. "You were wrong and you lost. I have three points and you have two." He held me against his chest as I cried. He rubbed the back of my head softly. "Shh, amore. It will be fine." He grabbed my chin forcing me to look at him. "It's fine, he will live." He leaned closer to me pressing a quick kiss on my lips. "You'll get used to it. We have two more days to play."

He walked past me and I stood there. I was scared, sick, and confused. Why was he making me play this game? Was he trying to punish me? Was he trying to scar me for life? I knew that what my brother did to him was serious, but this was insane. He said that I would be okay, but I didn't see how. This was way more than what I expected, and it terrified me. I wasn't going to make it through another day of this.

I hope you all enjoyed this chapter

RUSH & ROULETTE 2

It was time to play the second round of rush and roulette and I wasn't ready. I was scared because I didn't know what to expect. Who would we hurt this time? Why were these men being hurt in the first place? I didn't want my brother to be in a situation like this and so I had to play. I didn't need to just play, I had to win. I lost the last round and so I needed to be sure that I won this round. Vain walked into the room and I took a step back. He noticed instantly and smirked, I hated when he did that. He loved to see that I was scared of him, and I needed to stop giving him that satisfaction. He picked up the gun and handed it to me. I took it quickly and waited for them to bring out another man. I didn't have to wait long because a minute later they were dragging a man into the room. He was covered in blood and his face was beaten badly. I had to look away to stop myself from gagging. What the hell did he do to this man, beat him with a bat? Vain clapped his hands and I frowned. Ugh, he was enjoying this, and it made me sick. He walked over to the guy and grabbed a fistful of his hair yanking it back. I could see the fear in his eyes, and it hurt me. He looked at me as if begging me to help him. I closed my eyes tight but opened them quickly when I heard Vain speak.

"Meet our little friend, Nathan. He has been a bad boy and he is going to be punished. So, today we get to see if he lives or dies."

I wrapped my arms around myself protectively. "Vain, I can't. I don't want to hurt anyone else."

"Well, if it makes you feel better, he hurt a woman. He killed her actually ...well after raping her."

I gasped and covered my mouth. People like that really existed? Was that the type of thing that happened in the mafia?

"You see, the world isn't all butterflies and rainbows, Aya. We punish men so that they either learn a lesson or they die. You don't commit crimes like that in the mafia unless you are told to. I told him to go get the man that stole from me and he decided to change the rules. He raped his wife and then killed her. That wasn't what I told him to do and now we have cops asking questions. He made more trouble for me than what I wanted, so he will be punished. Now, let's start the game because I have a meeting to go to."

Knowing what he did made me feel better about hurting him, but it still bothered me. I walked over to him and pointed the gun at his foot. Vain chuckled and said No bullet and I pulled the trigger. The gun clicked, and Vain clapped his hands. I handed him the gun and he pointed it at the guy's knee. I said no bullet and he pulled the trigger. Once again, the gun clicked, and he passed it back to me. I pointed the gun at his hand and Vain said bullet. I pulled the trigger and the gun clicked. He was wrong and so that earned me a point. When he took the gun from me, he pointed it at his head. I knew that there was a bullet in this round. I didn't know how, but I knew what was coming.

"Bullet," I whispered. He pulled the trigger and the gun went off. I covered my ears and squeezed my eyes closed. I could feel his blood splatter on my skin and it made me sick. I covered my mouth and clutched my stomach. I felt the vomit creeping up, and I hated it. I couldn't stop the tears from sliding down my cheeks. I couldn't control the heart-wrenching sobs that slipped past my lips. The room was spinning and I felt like I was going to faint.

"It's okay," he whispered lifting me into his arms. "Calm down, you're having a panic attack." He looked over his shoulder at his men, "pulisci questo." (Clean this up) He walked out of the old cellar, and when the fresh air hit my nose I felt like I could breathe again. He sat me down on my feet and I pushed him away.

"WHY ARE YOU DOING THIS? WHY ARE YOU TORTURING PEOPLE LIKE THIS? WHAT GIVES YOU THE RIGHT TO TAKE A LIFE! YOU ARE FUCKED UP IN THE HEAD. DO YOU KNOW THAT?"

I couldn't control the words that were slipping past my lips. I despised him more than anything. He was sick in the head and it was showing. He tried to reach for me but I slapped his hand away.

"What is the matter with you? You are insane! I'm going to the police right now."

He reached for me again and I tried to stop him, but he grabbed me by the hair and pulled me close. "If you think about going to the police, you will regret it. You need to calm down."

"Go to hell," I snapped back staring into his eyes.

He stared at me for a second before laughing. "There is that feisty side of you that I wanted to see. I think it's cute to be shy and innocent, but I like my women feisty."

"I don't give a damn what you like. I don't like you and I'm not here to like you. I'm here to save my brother."

He pulled on my hair harder causing me to gasp. "You will be whatever I want you to be, Aya. You are mine and I will do whatever I want to you. And guess what, you will do whatever I tell you because you want to save your brother. Don't forget who I am. I can take everything from you including your life."

"You wouldn't kill me," I whispered challenging him.

He raised an eyebrow, "what makes you think that?"

"Because you told Aito that you wouldn't hurt me, that's what you said. You are a man of your word, right?"

"I am, but that doesn't mean that I don't have other ways to punish you, Aya."

"Why are you so evil?" I couldn't stop the words from slipping past my lips.

"Because I have to be. I'm a nice guy once you get to know me, but you are getting on my bad side. I have to show people that they can't do whatever the hell they want. I am the boss and I make the rules. It is my job to put fear into people's hearts, it's what I've been doing my whole life."

I knew that it was true. It was his job to be a ruthless Mafia leader. He was doing his job well, but it turned him into a monster. He was a beautiful man, and I knew that he had a heart. He was giving my brother a second chance, so why was he so bitter?

"Are you happy?" I was curious to hear his answer.

"No," he whispered brushing his lips against mine. "I will never be happy, Aya. Happiness was taken from me when I was a child."

Before I could say another word he captured my lips in a heated kiss. It took my breath away and surprised me at the same time. I wanted to pull away, but I couldn't. Something about him was pulling me in, and it scared me. He made me feel angry but hot at the same time. I hated his hands on me, but I loved it at the same time. Why was this happening? Was I still shaken up from what happened a minute ago? Was I losing my mind or was he just good at pulling women in? As I got lost in his kiss I couldn't find the answer.

I decided to take a shower because I needed to wash the blood off me. It was making me nauseous just smelling it. I stood under the hot water and enjoyed the feeling of it against my skin. I watched as the blood mixed with the water and ran down the drain.

I wasn't used to being in Vain's house and he still hadn't given me my cellphone. I knew that I had a lot of texts and calls from Kimi. If I played by his rules and showed him that he could trust me maybe he would give me my phone. I grabbed the body wash and washed my body quickly. I was tired and the bed was calling my name. I finished my shower and dressed for bed quickly. I walked out of the bathroom and jumped back in surprise when I saw Vain sitting on the bed. He was holding my phone in his hand.

"I'm going to give this to you, but you can not mention where you are. You won't tell anyone anything about what is going on. Do you understand?"

I nodded my head quickly and he stood up making his way towards me. I caught sight of the tattoo again and I frowned. Those were my initials or did they belong to someone else?

He chuckled, "what are you looking at?"

I tucked a strand of hair behind my ear, "you have an A and V on your chest. What does it mean?"

He stared at me for a second before smiling. "Do you really want to know?"

I hesitated for a minute before nodding my head slowly. My eyes never left his as he towered over me.

"The A stands for Athena. The V stands for Vintalli. The sunflower represents her family sign."

I frowned, that name sounded familiar. When I was in school I went to school with a girl named Athena. She loved to dance and she was so beautiful. She was a senior and I was a junior. Everyone always told me that we looked alike, but I didn't believe them. I always thought that she was way prettier than me. She was sweet, outgoing, and full of sunshine. She was the nicest person that you would ever meet and I hated that we didn't become friends. Her brother Roman was so sexy and half of the junior class had a crush on him.

"I know her," I whispered. "We went to school together."

He stared at me in shock before smiling, "it's a small world after all. What do you know about her?"

"Not much, she was the prettiest senior in her class. Everyone loved her and she was so down to earth. How do you know her?"

He chuckled, "do you really want to know."

I hated when he did that. He knew that I wanted to know so why was he asking? "Yes."

He leaned in close and I trembled, feeling his breath on my neck. "I took her virginity."

I gasped and tried to push him away but he pinned me to the wall. "She was supposed to be with me, but she wasn't fully Italian. So, I was going to keep her as my little toy, but things didn't go as planned."

"Did you hurt her?" I asked before I could stop myself.

"No, she managed to get away from me. Now, she is married, has a son, and lives in California."

I was relieved to hear that she was safe. I wasn't expecting him to tell me that he took her virginity, but it made sense. Athena always loved sunflowers. She would wear them in her hair and she had a sunflower purse she carried all the time. I thought that it complimented her well, I didn't know it was her family sign.

"I'm glad that she's okay."

"It seems like you were very fond of her."

I smiled, "we had a lot in common."

"Well, now you and I have a lot in common." He grabbed my breast and I gasped. "Athena is not what you think she is. She is a slut who took something from me. Do you want to know what it was?"

I was scared now. My heart was hitting my chest hard as he stared into my eyes. "What did she take?"

"She took my heart and never gave it back. She let another man have what belonged to me, and I will never forgive her for that."

"But you tattooed her initials on your chest. That must mean."

"It means nothing." He cut me off. "It's a constant reminder to me to never get close to another woman again. She destroyed me from the inside out. I will never allow her to be happy because I can't have that."

If I wasn't scared before, I was definitely scared now. Athena was a sweet girl, but he hated her. I could see the anger in his eyes. I could feel his rage pouring out of him like water. "You want to punish her," I whispered.

He laughed, "punish her...no...I want her, but I can't have her. Do you know how frustrating it is to desire something so badly but you can't have it? It's like being allergic to chocolate but you desire the taste of a brownie."

I didn't want to ask any more questions because I feared his answers. He was not happy with Athena moving on, and I could see that. But why would she give him her virginity just to move on? None of it made sense to me. Who was she married to and why was he so bitter about it? If he took her virginity that meant that he was with her at one point. Did she leave him because she saw his true colors? That had to be it because there was no other explanation.

I hope you all enjoyed this chapter

ADD UP

We played another round of rush and roulette and now it was time to add up our points. Vain had won the first round. He finished with three points and I finished with two. The second time we played, I finished with three points and he finished with one. The third time that we played I finished with two points and he finished with one. I was happy that the third game was over quickly. I was the one who had to shoot the man this time, and I hated it. It was his foot, so he would live, but it was still gruesome. I wanted this to be over but I still had nine more games to play with him. I didn't know what the next game would be and I didn't want to find out. Knowing what I knew about Athena made me sad. I wanted to know more about her but I was scared to ask. He said that he didn't hurt her, but I didn't trust him.

"So, you have seven points and I have five points. You won the first game, Aya."

I looked up and forced a smile, "that's great." I was happy that I managed to win, but it didn't calm my nerves. I got lucky, but the next game probably wouldn't be a game of luck. What the hell was I going to do when it came down to a game that I didn't know how to play? I couldn't think like that, I had to stay focused.

"I'll give you two days to rest and then we will be moving on to our second game."

I nodded my head and walked towards the stairs. I was tired and I needed a shower. It was the only thing that was going to help me relax. I wanted to talk to Aito again, but I knew that I was at his mercy. Even though I was able to talk to Kimi, I felt sad. I couldn't tell her what was going on, and she was angry with me. She thought that I was upset about her going off to Harvard, and that's why I didn't see her before she left. But that wasn't true, so I had to make up a good excuse. I told her that I had a family emergency, and she seemed to believe it. Now that I was back in my room, I felt good. I felt relieved to be away from Vain, but I wanted to go home. I had left everything behind to come here with him. I know that my job was worried sick about me, but there was nothing I could do. I was able to call my boss, but he was upset. He said that I should have still called, but I couldn't. He told me not to worry about coming back which hurt me. Ugh, all of this was Aito's fault. Why was he getting himself mixed up with a guy like this anyway? Was he out of his mind? As I undressed, I couldn't stop thinking about the amount of money that he owed Vain.

"You're sexy."

I turned around and gasped when I saw Vain leaning against the door. How long had he been standing there? I tried to cover myself with my hands, but it wasn't working. "What are you doing in here?"

He smirked, "this is my house and no room is off-limits." He took a step towards me and I backed away. What was he trying to do?

"Get out."

"What will you do if I don't?" He asked continuing to walk towards me. I backed away until my back hit the wall. He wasted no time caging me in so that I couldn't escape. I stared down at my feet, afraid to look at him. "You have a beautiful body, Aya. Has anyone ever seen you naked?"

"No," I whispered, feeling his hand on my thigh. "Please, stop."

He stared at me for a minute before forcing me to look at him. "Do you want me to take it? I'll make you into a woman just like I did your little friend."

"No, you won't have my virginity. Just because you managed to get hers doesn't mean anything."

He chuckled, "I don't want it anyway. The last thing I need is another woman attached to me."

I stared at him in disgust, "I wouldn't ever give it to you. I don't know why she did, I'm guessing she didn't know who you really were."

He shrugged, "say what you want, but she was begging me for more. I don't have to lie about that. She even agreed to marry me. So, I don't think she was upset about it."

"You must have brainwashed her because there is no way that Athena would fall for you. She was too smart to get caught up with a man like you."

"Athena was my piccolo puttana. She begged me to fuck her and I gave her that. You can believe what you want, but Athena was not what you think. She was sweet and innocent on the outside, but she was a slut on the inside."

I couldn't stop myself from slapping him across the face. My hand stung from the impact and the room was deathly silent. I stood there watching as he moved his jaw up and down slowly. "Don't talk about her like that. You are just upset because she didn't love you." I didn't know where all this courage was coming from, but I liked it. I wasn't about to sit here and allow him to talk about Athena like that. She wasn't my friend, but I knew her. She didn't deserve to be talked about like this. "You will not degrade her; I won't allow it."

He grabbed my hand and pinned me to the wall roughly. "Don't hit me, I promise you will regret it. She is not here to protect you. Stop trying to act like a fucking hero because you won't win against me. You will not change my mind about a woman that I knew since she was a baby."

He walked out of the room leaving me standing there alone. I didn't mean to hit him, and I didn't know why I got so upset about Athena.

VAIN

I paced back and forth slowly. Ever since I left Aya in her room, I couldn't stop thinking about Athena. Her words were stuck in my head.

"Don't talk about her like that. You are just upset because she didn't love you."

Was that the truth? Was I upset because she didn't love me? She did love me and I know that she did. But why was she so happy to go skipping back to him? Why did she go back to Satoni? I knew that I was the one who put his child into her and it wasn't supposed to be that way. I ran my fingers through my hair and downed my drink in one gulp. I was growing more irritated by the second. A knock sounded at the door and I said come in. My therapist walked in and smiled at me. She was wearing a short black skirt, a white button-up shirt, and black stiletto heels. Her long black hair flowed down her back, just like Athena's. I was surrounding myself with women who reminded me of her. She sat down and crossed her legs before clearing her throat softly.

"So, let's talk about what's going on. The last time I saw you, we talked about Athena. Have you figured out why you feel the way you do about her?"

"No," I said pouring myself another glass.

"Okay, well we need to understand why you feel the way you do. So, let's play a little game. I say a word and you tell me the first thing that comes to your mind."

I didn't know how this was going to help me, but I was willing to try. "Okay," I mumbled before downing my drink.

"Sunflower."

"Athena," I said sitting down.

"Athena."

I closed my eyes and leaned back. "mine."

"Black."

"Hair," I responded.

"Tainted," she continued.

"Blood." I opened my eyes and turned to face her. "How is this helping me?"

She smiled, "because you're thinking about Athena. Your thoughts are consumed with her. So, why don't you tell me where things went wrong with you and Athena?"

"She isn't fully Italian. That's where things went wrong."

She frowned, "but why does it matter?"

"Because my family is pure blood and we don't marry outsiders."

"Who told you that? Is that something that you decided or is that a family thing?" She asked pulling out her notebook.

"My father told me that," I sighed.

"Okay, but if you could have it your way, would you be with her?"

I sat there for a minute thinking about it. If I could have things my way would I be with her? The answer to that question was yes. I didn't care that she was mixed. I loved her, and I wanted to be with her. "Yes, I would be with her."

She started to write on her notepad, "why did you put his baby inside her? If you loved her, why would you want to put her through that kind of pain?"

My jaw clenched, "It wasn't my idea. I wanted her, but I couldn't have her. I knew that I would be going to war with my father if I got her pregnant. So, I accepted the help that was offered to me. I wasn't expecting her to find out, and once she did she ran back to him."

"So, what were your plans with her?"

"Keep her to myself. I couldn't marry her legally, but as long as she believed it, I was happy." I knew that sounded selfish of me, but it was true.

"But you knew that she was going to find out one day. So, why risk it? They say if you love something, you should set it free."

I stood up and smiled, "I did. I let her go free and before I knew it, she was falling in love with him. I knew that I had to get her back, and so I flew out to California."

She continued to scribble words on the paper. "What is it about her that drives you crazy? You say that you love her but then you say that you hate her. You say that she is nothing but a slut, but then you say she is yours. Why do you feel so many emotions towards her? We have to understand your feelings before we can discover the root of the issue. So, let's go back into your past. You said there was a woman that you loved. She was killed by Satoni, right? Can you tell me how you felt about her?"

I started to pace back and forth in front of her slowly. "She was the first woman that I ever loved. Her name was Isabella Perez. She was the first woman that my parents liked. I thought that we would be together, but it didn't work out. You know that story so I won't go over the graphic details of her death."

She sat back slowly, "does Athena remind you of her?"

"No, Athena looks more like her younger sister Alondra."

She placed her hand on her chin, "you started dealing with Athena to get back at Roman. Do you think that while you were spending time with her, you fell in love?"

"No," I smirked.

"Do you think it was because she was a virgin? You said that she was the second virgin that you had. Do you think that maybe you developed this claim over her?"

"No," I said walking over to my bar to get another drink. "You know what, why don't you tell me what you think. You keep asking me the same questions every week, and my answers don't change. So, tell me what you think."

She sat up slowly, "I think...that you love her. You love her and you hate that you do. Athena was supposed to be your one-way ticket to get back at Satoni. You thought that if you took her virginity, you would be able to get even with him. But your plan backfired because you ended up falling in love with her. You knew that you couldn't be with her because she wasn't rightfully yours, and she had tainted blood. But you decided that you didn't care about the rules, and you wanted to be with her anyway. The more time that you spent with her, the more you started to care. Every time you looked at Athena, you saw Isabella, and you never wanted to see Athena like that. So, you started to push her away because you wanted to keep her safe. Then, when you saw that it wasn't working, you decided to hire the Alba Rossa to kidnap her. You thought that if you did that, you could prove to yourself and your father that you didn't love her. But when Blue attacked her that night, you got upset. You started doing what you always do and started to push her away. When she got taken by Satoni, you let her go. You felt like you did what you wanted to do, but you couldn't seem to let her go. You thought that seeing her with another man wouldn't bother you, but it did. You wanted what was best for her, but that dominant part of you couldn't seem to let her go. You took her virginity and so you felt like you owned her. No matter how hard you tried to tell yourself that you didn't love her, you kept trying to find ways to keep her in your life. When she started to desire you again, you moved her to Seattle. You thought that if she was away from you and Satoni, her life would be better. But once again you found yourself wanting her, and so you leaked her address to Satoni. You thought that if Satoni got her back that would keep you away from her. But once again your plan backfired because she came searching for you looking for a way out. You had sex with her, but you knew that you couldn't be with her. So, you put his sperm in her. You hoped that she would realize that she was pregnant by him, and stay with him, but you didn't know that she hadn't had sex with him yet. She came to you thinking the baby was yours, and you ran with it instead of being honest. You wanted to continue to punish Satoni, you loved that she kept choosing you over him. But your plan backfired again, and she started to hate you. But that's what you wanted though. You wanted her to carry

Satoni's baby because then you could force her to be with him. You wanted her to be with a mafia leader so that you knew that she would always be safe. You wanted her to hate you so that she could move on, but you can't stop thinking about her. You call her all these names because you think it will help you get over her, but it doesn't work that way. You love her, and you should admit it."

I stared at her for a second before gulping my drink down. The alcohol burned my throat and I clenched my teeth. "That's...a bunch of bullshit," I muttered walking out of the room. I didn't love Athena, and I never did. I only wanted her virginity and family resources.

I hope you all enjoyed this chapter

A DEVIL

VAIN

I stared down at Isabella's head in the box and I couldn't stop myself. How could they do this to her? My heart felt like it had been ripped out of my chest. I couldn't breathe and I was blinded by rage. I grabbed my gun and walked towards the door quickly. My father grabbed me before I could leave. Why was he stopping me? I was going to kill Satoni's ass, and he couldn't stop me. There was nothing that he could do to me anymore. He took away the one thing that made me happy, and now I was going to kill his sorry ass.

"I'm going to make him regret this shit."

My father pushed me down on the couch. "I know that you're angry, but you have to be smart. Keep your head in the game because if you don't you'll end up dead. He wanted blood for what you did to his sister and now he got it."

"I DIDN'T KILL HER!"

He grabbed me by the collar, "watch your tone. I told you that this lifestyle is not for women. If you decide to have a wife, remember that she will be used against you. You knew that when you started dealing with her. If you want to blame someone, blame yourself. You're the one who left her with no protection. You know that you are supposed to leave her with security."

He was right, I had fucked up. I left her unprotected and that gave them the opportunity to kidnap her. It was my fault that she was dead, but I still wanted to kill them.

"I won't let you start a war over a girl."

"She wasn't any girl; she was the love of my life. She was carrying my baby and they murdered her. Do you have any idea what I'm going through right now? I don't think you do because you have the woman that you love."

He sighed running his fingers through his hair, "you're right. I don't know what it's like, but that doesn't change the rules. If she was your wife, it would be different, but she wasn't. She was a girl that you were fucking and you caught feelings. Move on and get over it because we will get them back."

"How?" I asked tucking my gun in my waistband.

He handed me a drink and I took it. "They have a container of cocaine heading to Texas. We are going to take it; they will lose six hundred thousand."

"That sounds good," I mumbled downing my drink in one gulp.

He smirked and patted me on the shoulder, "I'm placing you in charge. Kill as many of their men as possible. That will be your revenge, and you know you only get one shot."

"I won't mess it up, I'll take advantage of this." I stood up and my mom walked into the room. I knew that she didn't like when I went on missions like this, but she had to understand that I needed to do this.

"Vain, I don't think this is a good idea."

"Mom, I'm not in the mood for a lecture right now. I need to handle this and I will. Did you see what they did to her?"

She sighed, "yeah. But you know that killing will never make things right. It won't bring her back."

"They started this war, and I'm going to finish it." I walked out of the room before she could say another word. There was no way that they were going to get away with this.

When I arrived at the location where the drop was being made, I was surprised to see Roman with his father. The Romano family had them picking it up? What the hell was going on? I sat in my car and watched as Roman and his father joked with each other. I couldn't stop the surge of jealousy that surged through me. They always had a good relationship, and I was envious of it. Roman was eighteen and he had grown to be tall just like his dad. He looked just like his father, but he had his mother's smile. They weren't even treating this like a mission as I watched them play wrestle. That was the one thing that I hated about their family. They were pure, not an ounce of evil in them. Why couldn't my family be like that? The trucks started to arrive and my men and I started to prepare to shoot, but I stopped when I noticed a girl walking towards them. She was yelling at them and I couldn't make out what she was saying. I held my hand up to hold off my men. Why was a girl here and who was she? She was wearing a pair of short denim shorts, a white crop top, and white and black Dior sneakers. Her long black hair was blowing in the wind as she made her way over to them. She was young, but she was so beautiful and her body was already very developed.

"DAD, HURRY UP!" She screamed placing her hand on her hip. "I'M HUNGRY AND YOU PROMISED ME PIZZA."

Roman jogged over to her quickly, "dad is busy. We told you to wait in the car. We will be there in a minute."

She rolled her eyes, "ugh what are you two doing anyway? I've been waiting for ten minutes."

He shoved her, "go wait in the car. Don't come back."

"You're not the boss of me," she snapped back.

Alonzo walked over to them and wrapped his arms around them. "Both of you stop it now. Athena, go wait in the car, sunshine. I promise I'm coming." She sighed loudly and turned around making her way towards the car that was a distance away.

Athena...that was Athena? I hadn't seen her since she was a baby. She was gorgeous, she had really grown into her looks. She looked just like her mom, and her smile took my breath away.

"Vain, what are you doing? We need to go ahead and get the trucks."

I turned to look at Ace and shook my head slowly. "No, the mission is off."

He stared at me confused, "what the hell? What are you talking about? Your dad is going to be pissed if we don't get these trucks."

I started the car, "I said the mission is off. Don't question me about it."

He sat back in his seat and mumbled something that I couldn't understand. I knew that if we opened fire, they would die. Even though I wanted to make Satoni suffer, I couldn't kill Alonzo. I wouldn't kill him in front of his kids. I was pissed off but I wasn't evil. Besides, my issue wasn't with the Vintalli family, it was with Satoni and his people. The Vintalli's were in the wrong place at the wrong time. But I had a feeling that Satoni did it on purpose.

My father slammed his hand down on the desk. I knew that he was going to be angry that I canceled his mission, but I didn't care. I couldn't stop thinking about Athena. Damn, she had to be about fifteen now, right? I placed my hand on my chin and thought about it. When was the last time I had seen them? Athena was about one year old, had it been that long?

"Are you listening to me?"

I raised an eyebrow, "yeah." I wasn't but I was telling him what he wanted to hear.

"Why the hell did you cancel the mission?"

"Because Alonzo was there and he had Roman with him."

He frowned, "so what? They are the enemy as well, have you forgotten that?"

I sighed, "no. But Athena was there too. I wasn't about to kill him in front of his daughter. She's only fifteen, and she didn't need to see something like that."

He stared at me for a second before laughing, "are you serious? You stopped my mission because of a little girl. Vain, where the hell is your head at right now? You aren't thinking clearly."

I leaned back in my chair and tried to keep my temper under control. "I did what I felt was the best thing to do. You said yourself that we can't go around creating unnecessary wars. They are not the enemy right now but killing them would start one. My issue is with Satoni, not with some third party that works for him."

"I gave you an order," he growled.

"I'm not about to have that kind of blood on my hands. If you want it so badly go kill him. But I want no parts of it. I'm glad that I saw her when I did because she would have been dead."

He stared at me for a second before sitting down in his chair. "I feel like it was stupid what you did, but I trust your decision and quick thinking. Alonzo isn't an enemy of ours and he is very resourceful. Besides, he still has two parts of New York. So, that means that we have to get along with him for now. I hate that Satoni did that shit though. He knew what we had planned and planned in advance. He is a smart kid; I'll give him that. His father left him in charge and showed him all the loopholes."

"He has what is coming to him, I can guarantee you that."

My father frowned, "you said that Athena was there, right?"

"Yeah, why?"

"You know that is Satoni's soon-to-be bride," he smirked.

I sat up quickly, "what? How do you know?"

"I'm a mafia leader, Alonzo told me. He said that he wanted Athena to be safe when she reached the age of eighteen. So, he decided that once Athena turns eighteen, she will be Satoni's wife."

I gripped the arm of the chair trying to calm myself down. "I never thought that he would make a decision like that."

"It makes sense. We need to make sure that the little girl doesn't go tainting any more mafia bloodlines. I think it will be best for her to be with Satoni. You know that he is tainted blood too. They can make filthy blooded babies and we can rest easy knowing she is with him. It's a win-win situation."

I shook my head, "I think it's stupid. If they get married they will have access to even more resources. That would make the Romano family even stronger and richer."

He laughed, "you don't miss a thing. But that works to our advantage. You wanted revenge and you will have your revenge."

"What do you mean?"

"Why don't you enjoy his bride before he does. Imagine if you were her first, he would never be able to change that. Making her fall in love with you is the best revenge for him. Taking something that rightfully belongs to him is the best way to get back at him."

I smiled and nodded my head slowly, "I see what you're saying."

One thing about my father was the fact that he was smart. He always wanted to destroy people from the inside out. He thought that death was too easy. He wanted to do things to people that would last them a lifetime. I thought that it was a good idea at the time, and I decided to do it. He took something from me and so I would do the same to him. I never hurt his sister, but he was too blind to see that. Now, he was going to regret taking Isabella from me. I would have gotten married and changed to be a better man for her. But now that she was gone...I was reborn.

I was a devil...and I loved it.

I hope you all enjoyed this chapter

SEX DICE

I t was time to play the second game and I was nervous. I walked into his game room and he was sitting down at the table. I didn't hesitate to sit down across from him. I was happy that we were playing a game where no one would get hurt this time. But I still felt nervous about what we were going to be doing. He gulped down his drink and looked at me.

"Today we will be playing a dice game. This game is simple and I'm sure you will enjoy it."

I was happy that he said that because he didn't mention me loving the previous game. Maybe luck was on my side this time, but I couldn't get my hopes up.

"You will have a dice and I will have one. The dice each have words on them. Now, I will roll my dice and you will roll yours. Whatever they land on, that's the action that we have to do. If you choose not to do it, you lose. We will keep track by having points for each action that we do. Does this make sense to you?"

"Yes," I picked up my dice and observed it. My dice had body parts listed on it. Hand, feet, neck, what did that mean? I couldn't stop my heart from skipping a beat. Was he going to hurt me or make me hurt him?

I'll let you go first since you won the last game."

I gulped but rolled the dice quickly. It rolled across the table for what seemed like forever before finally landing. When I leaned close to see what it landed on, it said lips. I frowned and he chuckled rolling his dice. It landed on kiss. I sat back in my chair slowly. What the hell did that mean?

"It seems you have earned yourself a kiss, Aya."

My eyes widened when I realized what this game was. He leaned in and so did I. A simple kiss wouldn't hurt besides, it could have been worse. He grabbed me by the hair and slammed his lips against mine. I gasped and he took that as an opportunity to slip his tongue into my mouth. I was lost in the kiss instantly and he used that to his advantage. When he finally pulled away, I could tell that he was satisfied. I was breathing heavily and my skin was hot. He leaned back and so did I. It was his turn now. He picked up his dice and rolled it quickly. It landed on the word suck and he chuckled. It was up to me to roll something simple, so I picked up my dice and rolled. It landed on finger and I sighed in relief. He rubbed his thumb across my bottom lip and I opened my mouth so that I could suck it. He groaned, and I had to stop myself from throwing up. I couldn't believe that I was stuck doing this. When he pulled his thumb away from my mouth, I was happy. He picked up his dice and rolled it and I did the same. My dice landed on breast and his dice landed on touch. I sighed; damn he would have to touch my boobs. He didn't waste any time grabbing it roughly and rubbing it. I guess he was eager to keep the game going because he pulled his hand away and rolled his dice. His landed on kiss and when I rolled mine it landed on neck. He leaned his head over to the side allowing me access to his tattooed neck. I leaned in slowly and started to suck on his neck gently. I wasn't sure what I was doing because I had never done it before. Was he enjoying it or did he hate it because I was inexperienced? When I caught myself thinking about it, I pulled away. Why did I care if he enjoyed it or not? He picked up his dice and rolled it and I did the same. His landed on the word lick and mine landed on clit. I gasped and jumped out of my seat. There was no way that I was going to allow him to do that to me. He stared at me with an amused look on his face.

"What's wrong? Are you giving up?"

"Yes, there is no way that I'm going to let you do that to me." I crossed my arms over my chest.

"Then I win the game. We will play again tomorrow and we will see who will be victorious." I turned to leave but was pulled back. I tried to get my arm free from his steel grip, but I failed. What the hell was he doing? The game was over and he won so why was he keeping me here?

"What are you so afraid of?" he whispered into my ear.

"I'm not afraid of anything."

"You're lying," he smirked, sucking my earlobe into his mouth. I moaned softly and pushed against his chest. "Let me help you relax," he whispered, lifting me onto the pool table. "I mean you wore this dress for a reason. You wanted to tease me and now you have. So, let me tease you, Aya. I'm going to show you how you make me feel."

Slowly, almost without me noticing, he slipped my panties over my smooth thighs, pulling them away from one of my legs. He pulled my legs apart with ease despite my struggling to expose my damp center.

"Vain, what are you doing?" I didn't want to do this with him. I wanted to say no but as he stared at me, I couldn't get the words to come out.

"You have a beautiful body," he whispered caressing my thigh. "I want to worship you, will you let me, amore?"

I bit my lip trying to fight the urge to moan. His voice was sexy and filled with lust. The way he stared at me made me crave him more. He was sexy as hell and he wanted to pleasure me. It didn't make sense to me; I mean I wasn't nearly as pretty as the women he had. I blushed as I felt his nails scraping softly down my skin. He pushed me back and I stared up at the ceiling. I could feel him kissing me gently and I trembled. I wanted to see what he was doing. The thought of him exploring me down there caused me to prop myself up on my elbow. I felt his breath against my core, the wetness between my legs began to build as our eyes met. I shook my head suddenly, my mind putting the pieces together as he began to slide his tongue over my slightly spread lips. My body shivered in response, and he paused to spread my legs wider apart. I shuddered, and he smirked biting his lip.

"You taste good."

"D-Don't say stuff like that." I gasped, trying to pull my legs out of his monstrous grip.

My resistance dissolved as his tongue curled around my swollen clit. His tongue was pushing its way into my tight opening. My legs gave a great shiver, and my hips rolled forward towards the intrusion. It slowly worked deeper inside of me, drawing my sweet juices out with slow, tender strokes. He cupped my butt, his nails slowly digging into my skin. I moaned loudly clutching the table for support. I had never felt like this before, and I couldn't deny it felt amazing. He held me tight so that I couldn't escape him. He didn't give me time to catch my breath, his tongue never paused as it went deeper inside of me. It felt as though lightning struck through me, never had I experienced anything so intense. He held me open as he kept returning to the spot that caused me to whimper and moan. His teeth teased me, his tongue lashed and probed me. Everything seemed to vanish as he took me in his mouth, sucking on my swollen nub of flesh. I moaned and thrashed, bucking against his mouth. An incredible tension built between my thighs, coiling until I thought I would die. He groaned, my body arching as scorching heat rushed over me. As I began to tighten around his tongue, he drew it out of me with a loud sucking noise. I let out a loud moan, my voice nothing but lust and frustration, the world-shattering orgasm that had been building in the pit of my stomach was suddenly torn away. I stared down at him as he smiled, my juices were covering his lips. Slowly, he licked his lips and that turned me on even more.

"What do you desire, Amore? Do you want more?"

Why was he playing with me like this? He knew that I wanted more, so why was he denying me? I was out of my mind right now and I wanted the ache to go away. I reached down and started to rub my clit slowly. His eyes followed and I could see how turned on he was by my actions.

"So, you aren't so innocent after all?" He chuckled.

"Vain," I whispered, picking up the pace. "Please," I moaned biting my bottom lip.

He pulled my dress down and ran his tongue over one of my nipples. It grew hard instantly when he sucked it into his mouth. I found myself panting, my body pushing upwards towards his touch desperately. As I continued to stroke myself quickly, he started to suck on my other nipple. My lust rose higher as he gently started to nibble on the erect bud. My eyes rolled back, and I screamed, feeling myself get closer. Not knowing what to hold on to, I cupped my aching breast. His eyes were dark with approval as I unconsciously teased myself.

"Do you want me, Amore?" he breathed against my flesh.

My body screamed for the release only he could give me, yet some instinct, one last drop of dignity, prevented me from uttering the words that would end this achy feeling.

"No, I whispered continuing to move my fingers faster. I squeezed my eyes closed as I felt him pull away. "I...I," I didn't know what to say.

"Let me help you," he chuckled replacing my fingers with his mouth. I cried out and grabbed his head pushing him forward.

"Ohh, yes," I breathed as he devoured me once again. The sound of his mouth against me drove me insane. I couldn't hold it in anymore and I didn't want to. With one final scream, I came undone. My body arched upward and I moaned his name repeatedly. The feeling was so satisfying, and breathtaking.

He stood up and smiled at me, "I win, Amore."

That's all he said before leaving me alone in the room. I lay there trying to catch my breath. I wasn't sure what had just happened, or why I lost control. What the hell did I do? Why did I let him pleasure me? I climbed off the table and started to fix myself up.

I hope you all enjoyed this chapter

SEX DICE 2

It was time to play another round of our dice game. I wasn't excited about it because of what happened yesterday. I knew that I had to get myself together and not succumb to the feelings that he gave me. As much as I wanted to hate Vain for everything that he was putting me through, I couldn't help but feel curious about him. I wanted to know why he was the way that he was, and maybe I would never know. But I felt like when the time is right, I would ask him to see if maybe he would talk to me. But for now, that was the last thing on my mind. I had to get ready for this game, and I had to keep my mind in the right place. I walked into the game room and he was sitting at the table ready for me. I already knew what was expected of me so I picked up my dice, and I rolled it. It landed on the word ear. He rolled his dice and it landed on the word lick. I moved my hair over to the side allowing him access to my ear. I thought that he was going to be quick about it but he took his time. He made sure to drag his tongue slowly from the top of my ear to the bottom, and then he sucked my earlobe in to his mouth. I gasped, trying to keep myself together. I couldn't deny the fact that he made me nervous. He made me squeeze my legs together because I was anxious. He made me feel things that I hadn't felt in a long time.

"You were eager to play today," he chuckled.

"I just wanted to get it over with," I said quickly.

It was true, I wanted to get the game over with. If I played this round I would only have one more round left. The quicker that we got through with this game, the better it would be for me. I had no intention of having sex with him but I knew what foreplay led to. I picked up my dice and rolled it, it landed on lips. He picked up his dice and rolled it and it landed on the word kiss. It was my turn to kiss him this time. I leaned forward, and he smirked at me. If he was expecting me to tongue kiss him like he did me yesterday, he was wrong. I gave him a quick peck on the lips, and sat back in my seat. He seemed to be a little disappointed but I didn't care. I wasn't here to make out with him, I was here to win a game. Surprisingly, he didn't bother me about it though. He picked up his dice and rolled it with no hesitation. It landed on the word suck. I rolled my dice and to my surprise luck was not on my side. I stared down at the word penis in shock. There was no way that I was about to give him head. He stared at me for a minute, and I could see the amusement dancing across his face. He was happy because he knew that I was going to deny doing it. If I denied doing it, that meant that he would win another round. I knew that I had to win but we were only on our second game. I still had plenty of games to make up for this one. So, I decided that I would deny this round, and let him have the point.

"Are you going to deny me, Amore?"

"Yes, I stood up from the table quickly. I don't want to do that."

He chuckled, "I win."

"That's fine, I'll see you in the next round."

He laughed, "there won't be another round. I won two rounds out of three. Even if you did win the last round, It wouldn't change your fate. You lost the game and we don't need to play another round, and waste time when we already know the outcome."

He was right, there was no point in playing another round when he already won the two out of three. "Fine, you win this game."

He stood up and I backed away. The last thing that I needed was him doing what he did to me yesterday. I needed to make sure that he understood that I didn't want to have sex with him.

"Vain, I don't want to have sex with you. What happened yesterday was just because of the game. But I want to be clear about that. We are not going to have sex. No matter what you do to me, I won't give in. I want to keep my virginity."

"That's not true. You want to lose it, just not to me. If you came across the right man, you would open your legs with no hesitation. Besides, if I pleasured you enough, you would beg me just like you did yesterday."

"That will never happen again," I whispered.

"Never say never, Amore. I can eat you alive right here and you wouldn't do anything to stop me."

I wanted to deny him, but he was right. I couldn't seem to think straight when he touched me. I didn't know if that's because of how powerful he was or if I was attracted to him. I mean what woman wouldn't be. He was so sexy and everything about him pulled you in. From his long thick lashes to his grey eyes, and cocky attitude. He knew how to make women drop their panties for him.

"Well, I'm glad that we talked about this. I just wanted to make sure that you knew that I wasn't going to have sex with you."

He smirked, "I already told you that I don't want your virginity. I have no interest in fucking you, Aya. I like playing with your body because I like how it reacts to my touch but that's it. I don't desire to be with another virgin."

I didn't understand him at all. What did he have against virgins? Was this because of Athena? My curiosity got the best of me and so I asked him. I wasn't sure if he was going to respond, but I wanted to at least see what his response would be. "Why? Why don't you desire virgins? That's what most men want so what makes you so?"

He stared at me for a minute before smiling. "It's not that I don't desire my woman untouched. I don't desire the hassle that comes with a virgin. You get attached, and that's not something that I'm looking for right now. Besides, I've had my fair share of virgins and I'm over it. Every man has that faze where they want to fuck as many virgins as they can. But all I want is a feisty woman that knows how to please me. I like my women experienced, it's better that way."

"Does it have something to do with Athena?"

He frowned, "why does everything have to be about Athena? I already told you that she was nothing to me."

"I just have the feeling that that's not true. Something happened between you two and whatever it was is something that you can't get over."

"If you want to act like a therapist you should go to college and major in it. Nothing happened between the two of us. I wanted to fuck Athena and I did and that's all there is to it. I don't care what you think or anyone else thinks. I am the way I am because I'm Vain Grey. I get whatever the hell I want when I want and that includes women. The last thing that I would ever do is sit here and be in my feelings about one girl. She's one in a million, and she's definitely not the prettiest woman that I've ever fucked."

I sighed, "if you say so." I don't know who he was trying to convince, me or himself, but it wasn't working. He had some feelings that he didn't want to admit existed. It was only going to keep hurting him, and his relationships in the end.

He stepped towards me slowly, "what the hell is that supposed to mean?"

I backed away from him, "nothing."

"No, tell me how you feel. I want to know what you think about Athena and I."

He cupped my chin forcing me to look at him. "I don't know much about you. And I don't know much about Athena either, but I do know that she was a very sweet girl. I know that whenever I mention Athena or anyone around you for that matter, you get irritated. I'm not here to investigate what happened between the two of you. I am here to save my brother, and that's the only thing that I care about."

He brushed his lips against mine slowly. "Good, focus on that and that alone. I am not the kind of man that you want to get involved with. Don't get me wrong, Aya... I would fuck you. You have a body that is so beautiful and delicate, and I would ravish you. But I need you to understand that I would also destroy you at the same time. I am not a romantic type of guy and I never will be. No matter how much I try to play that part, my true colors always seep through. One thing that I learned about myself is that no matter how much I tried to love Athena, I couldn't. I will never be able to love her, and it was my mistake trying to. I thought that she would be my wife. I thought that I would be able to make him jealous, but it didn't work. He wanted her, she belonged to him, not me. I only wanted her for one thing and I got it. Athena is nothing to me, and she will never be. She was something nice to play with, and that's what I did."

"Be honest, you only wanted to keep Aito alive so that you could play with me. The only reason that you're doing this is because I look like her. You had a woman come over yesterday, and she looked similar to Athena. If you hate her so much, why are you constantly torturing yourself with her lookalikes?"

He smirked, "is that what you think? No...it's not torture, Aya. You see, I have a type and she is my type. It's not my fault that I keep getting lucky and stumbling across my type. But, I will be honest with you. I have no interest in you because you look like her. I will kill your brother and think nothing of it. I was trying to give him a second chance because I know that he is all you have. But don't think that I'm keeping him alive because you look like my ex. Even though you look like her, you will never be her."

We stood there for a moment not saying a word to each other. His lips were inches away from mine tempting me slowly. He was sexy but intimidating at the same time. He was strong but I knew that he had a weakness. He didn't want to admit it but his weakness was Athena. He walked away leaving me standing there alone. He was like a dark tunnel. I kept trying to find the light in him but there was none. He was dark, cold, and lonely. I didn't know if it started with Athena or not. But I had a feeling that it didn't. He had suffered some kind of heartbreak before her, and he thought that he could overcome it, but he couldn't.

I hope you all Enjoyed this chapter

ISABELLA

Isabella was sleeping in my arms and it was times like these that I felt like a normal person. Being with her brought me a lot of joy and I never had to worry about the mafia. She took away a lot of my reality. The only thing that I thought about was being with her, despite what my father thought. My mother loved Isabella and she thought that she was the best thing that happened to me. But my father didn't want me to get distracted by things that didn't matter, and he never hesitated to remind me. Isabella begin to stir and I knew that she would be opening her eyes soon. I wanted to propose to her. I knew that I wanted to spend the rest of my life with her. But I didn't want to ask her in a simple way. I wanted it to be special and it would be something that she remembers for the rest of her life. So, I decided that I will propose to her on her birthday. It would be the best gift that she would ever receive from me, and I knew she would be happy. She looked up at me and I smiled. I would never get tired of holding her in my arms.

"Is something wrong?"

"No, why would anything be wrong?" I asked kissing her head.

"I was just asking because you don't look like you got any sleep. You know if there's something on your mind, you can tell me."

"There's nothing on my mind. If there was, you know that you're the first person that I would talk to."

"Good, I'm glad to hear that. I have to go shopping today with Alondra because she needs to find a dress for her date. She was looking for something that's blue because that's his favorite color."

I smiled, "is she dating already?"

She sat up slowly and I couldn't stop my eyes from drifting down to her exposed chest. Her nipples were already erect and begging for me to suck on them. The thought of making love to her again caused me to get hard again. The things she did to me drove me crazy. She was so beautiful and I couldn't help but wonder if I really deserved her.

"Yes, she is a growing teenager and it's time that she started to date. I think that's a good idea, and the boy that she's going out with seems like a really nice guy. He makes her laugh and he spoils her."

I sighed, "okay. But I want you to take some security with you."

She rolled her eyes, "no. I hate when I have to drag those security guards around with me. They stick out in a crowd, and it's just not normal. People fear me when I walk around with them. They look mean all the time and they seem like they are ready to kill anyone who gets too close."

"Well, I'm not normal. I have enemies and I don't want anything happening to you."

She placed her hand on my chest, "nothing will happen to me. You're just being paranoid Vain. Besides, I'll be in the busiest part of the city. What could possibly go wrong in a crowded city? If anyone tries to get me, everyone will notice. It's only for one day and I'm sure that you can spare one day."

I didn't think it was a good idea despite her being in the busiest part of the city. I wanted to protect her but I also wanted to make sure that I was meeting her needs. It was a hard decision to make but I finally gave in and agreed.

"I'm going to call you every hour."

She giggled, "and if you don't call me I'll make sure to call you." She looked down at her hand and sighed. "I can't wait until one day we can be normal. I don't want our children to live like this."

I knew how she felt because she voiced it repeatedly. But there was no changing my fate and I wasn't about to let her go. I knew that sounded selfish, but I loved her more than my life, and I couldn't be without her, I wouldn't.

"I'm a mafia leader, Isabella. Our lives will never be normal and you know that. When we have a son, he will take over the head of the family. I can't change my fate because this was what I was born to do. My father is counting on me to take over after he is gone or too old to do so."

She tucked a strand of hair behind her ear. "I know, but sometimes I think that he puts too much pressure on you."

"It's his job. How about we change the subject? I would like to enjoy you a little while longer before you go shopping." I pulled her close, and she laughed slapping my arm playfully.

"You've enjoyed me long enough and besides I'm sore. I can only take so much," she whispered pressing her lips against mine. I pulled her close never wanting to let her go. She moaned into my mouth and climbed on top of me.

"I thought that you said that you were too sore," I chuckled watching as she rubbed herself against me.

"I am but you're so addicting that I can't help it."

I grabbed her and flipped us over quickly. She laughed and wrapped her arms around me pulling me close. I loved being like this with her.

"Vain, will you promise me something?"

I stared into her eyes, "yes."

"I want you to promise me that you will never love anyone more than me."

I smiled, "that's ridiculous. I could never love anyone more than I love you. You are my life and that will never change."

Her small hands cupped my face, dragging my mouth down to hers in an urgent kiss. My hand slid between our bodies, reaching down to her clit. I started to stroke her slowly, causing havoc between her quivering thighs. She placed her hand over mine demandingly, holding it where she desperately craved my touch.

Her body shuddered, her head spilling back, eyes rolling back, as I stroked her teasingly.

"Are you ready?" I groaned. I felt her heart picking up speed as she slowly nodded.

I thrust into her with one powerful stroke, stretching her tight walls around me as I slid inside of her to the hilt. My eyes gazed down into her wide ones as I slowly withdrew before ramming back into her, watching every expression flicker across her expressive face. She breathed a sigh of relief as I once again eased out of her, only to gasp as I thrust back inside her with more force. Her legs wrapped around me tightly, her hips were bucking to the pace I forced on her as my body slapped against her. She moaned my name and dug her nails into my back as I forced her to take each long stroke. I could feel her muscles clench instinctively around me, drawing a loud groan from me as she gripped me tightly. She was so addicting, and I loved watching her come undone.

"Tell me you love me," I whispered.

"I love you...I love you so much." She moaned.

"Vain, are you listening?"

I blinked a few times before finally realizing that I spaced out for a second. I turned to look at my therapist who was tapping her pen against her clipboard.

"Yes, I was listening."

"Okay, so what was the question that I asked you?"

I laid back on the sofa slowly. "Just ask me the question again."

She sighed, "I asked you how you felt about your mother."

"Well, I love my mom. She is my mother and she's always been there for me. What does this have to do with anything?"

"Well, you said that she's always been there for you. But once you turned fourteen, she left and went back to Spain, right?"

"Yeah, that's right." I didn't know where she was going with this but I would entertain it for now.

"Once your mother was gone, how did you feel? Did you feel lonely?"

"No, I knew that my mother wasn't happy in the United States. I was happy that she was able to go back to a place that she knew. When my mother came here, it was challenging for her. She never learned English fluently and she was miserable here. She stayed as long as she did because of me, but I knew that she would leave one day."

"What was your father like once she was gone?"

I shrugged, "nothing changed. He was the same man that he had always been my whole life. It wasn't until I was eighteen, and I was able to take over things in New York, that he went and got her."

She nodded her head slowly, "okay. So, you said that your father would cheat on your mother often. Was he cheating because he didn't want to be with your mother at that time?"

I sat up slowly, "I have no idea. If you want the answers to these questions maybe you should go be my father's therapist. I don't care about what he did or why he did it."

"Okay, I have two more questions for you and then we will be finished. Because your father was with multiple women, I can imagine that he wanted the same for you. Do you think that's the reason that you struggle to love is because of your father and what happened to Isabella?"

"Isabella plays a part and so does my father. My father always told me that love makes you weak. He wanted me to be at my best all the time."

"Was your father happy that Isabella was gone?"

I hesitated for a minute because it hurt to answer that question. "Yeah, he was happy that she was gone. He liked Isabella but he didn't like her for me. He said that she caused me to lose focus and he didn't want that."

I have one more question for you. "After you buried Isabella and Alondra, did you ever go back to visit them?"

"No."

"Why?" She whispered.

"Because they are dead. There's no point in going to visit bones. Besides, they are both in my past and I've moved forward."

"I would recommend going to visit them because that would be a big step in understanding your past. I also recommend that you embrace your true feelings about your mother and your father's relationship. But that's all for today and I'll see you next week." She stood up slowly and fixed her skirt before grabbing her briefcase.

"How do you know these things? How can you be so sure that will work? You don't think that maybe I was born to be this way?"

She turned around to face me, "no. The Vain that I see now is not the one that Isabella loved. I met you six months ago and I've already learned so much. But we will continue to talk and discover more."

She left the room quickly leaving me alone. Was she right? The more that I sat here and thought about it, it kind of made sense. I was happy when I was with Isabella. Now, I was filled with darkness. I had a lot of patience back then, but now I had none. I ran my fingers through my hair slowly. No, this was who I was meant to be. Isabella changed me, but that was only for a moment. In the end, whether she was still alive or not, I would be who I am today.

I hope you all enjoyed this chapter

3RD GAME

It was time for us to play our third game and I was happy because things were moving along very quickly. The quicker that I finished these games and won them, the sooner I could see my brother. I was still upset that he got us into this mess, but being mad at him wasn't going to help me. I kept reminding myself every day that I need to keep my head in the game, and I needed to stay focused. I walked into the room, and Vain was sitting at the table. He was wearing a black button-down shirt with black jeans. He seemed relaxed today, but I was nervous. My heart was pounding hard against my chest the closer that I got to him. I wasn't sure what game we would be playing and a part of me didn't want to know. I wasn't sure if it was going to be another game of violence or was there going to be some type of sexual act involved? He looked up at me and smiled and I rolled my eyes. I wasn't in the mood for his fake hospitality because that's all that it was. Vain was not a genuine person, and I wasn't about to fall for his tricks.

"I hope that you rested well because today our new game begins. Now this game is very simple and it will go by quickly as long as you play along."

I looked over when I saw his men dragging a man into the room. I stood up quickly because I knew that there was going to be blood. I hated that he was putting me through this. I hated seeing people hurt. He grabbed my arm and pulled me close. I should've known that he wasn't going to let me escape that easily.

"Where are you going? The game hasn't even begun and you're already trying to run away."

"Because I know what you're trying to do. I don't want to see anyone get hurt. This is torture and you know it. Why are you doing this?"

"He brushed my hair out of my face gently. This is not torture, this is the mafia. This is what happens to people who steal from me and lie to me. I want you to fully understand what will happen to your brother if you lose these games. I'm not doing this to torture you if that's what you think. Think of it as me teaching you and your brother a lesson. Now, I don't have all day so let's make this quick. I even decided to make this a one round game."

I was happy to hear that he was making this a one round game because that meant that we didn't have to play multiple rounds. All I had to do was get through this one round which was great, but it was challenging now. Because there was only one round, that meant that I only had one chance to win. If I lost this game, he would have two games against my one. I would still have quite a lot of time to catch up, but I didn't want him getting too far ahead of me. My brother's life was on the line and it was up to me to save him. There was no doubt in my mind that despite my discomfort, I had to go through this.

"What are the rules," I whispered. I was too afraid to ask but there was no point in dragging this out. He was going to do this whether I wanted him to or not and if I decided to forfeit the game, he would win. The only thing that I could do was play and hope for the best.

He smirked, "this game is another game where we are going to see if luck is on your side. I'm going to give you a dice and you are going to roll it. Now each number is going to represent one of his body parts. So, the number one represents his hand, two is his foot, three is his leg, four is his arm, five is his chest and six is his head. I am going to call out a number and then you were going to roll your dice. If your dice doesn't land on the number that I called out, you get a point. But if the dice lands on the number that I did call out, he gets shot. We are going to have four rounds. If I shoot him in his chest or his head, he will die. So, you need to understand that that means game over."

This game was stressful for sure. There were so many different scenarios playing in my head and it was distracting. This was a game of luck, and I could only hope that luck was on my side. I thought about trying to roll the dice in my favor, but would he notice? I knew that he said that he would not tolerate me cheating, so I couldn't risk it.

"Number four."

He grabbed his gun and walked over to the man that was tied to the chair. Thankfully, the man was blindfolded this time so at least I didn't have to look into his eyes as I decided his fate. I took a deep breath and closed my eyes before tossing the dice on the table. I heard it clatter against the glass before finally going quiet. I opened my eyes and stared down at the number five. I was relieved that I gained a point, and the man wouldn't be shot this round. But I still had three more rounds to get through. I looked at Vain and he smirked, he was enjoying this.

"Number three."

With shaky hands I picked up the dice and once again dropped it on the table. Once I heard it go quiet I opened my eyes, and I was once again relieved to see that I gained another point. The dice had four black dots indicating the number four. Two more rounds, that's all that I had left.

Vain was quick and didn't give me time to celebrate my victory. He called out the number one and I rolled the dice. This time I didn't close my eyes, I watched as it rolled around until it finally settled on the number two. The breath that I didn't realize I was holding was released. I hadn't realized how sweaty my palms were until I brushed them against my thighs. I was shocked when he didn't say a word. I looked over to see him tucking his gun in his waistband. He looked irritated and I didn't know why. Was something going on or was he just being an asshole?

You win this game. That's all he said before he left the room leaving me alone. I wanted to question him but I felt like it would be best if I didn't. I had no idea what he was thinking half of the time and that scared me. I couldn't help but think about who he truly was. He was strange and very hard to figure out. Why did he get off on inflicting pain on others? Why was he so bitter inside? I knew that he was a mafia leader and he had to be mean to some extent but he was extreme. Something inside of him was broken and sometimes he didn't even act human. The basic human emotions that we all have didn't seem to register with him. Who was Vain Grey? Why was he so distant and cold? It's like some days he would be in the mood to toy with me. Some days he would treat me as if I didn't exist. And then there would be some days that my very presents irritated him. Given the few conversations that we had, he never gave me any information. But today for some strange reason, I was in the mood to be more persistent. Without second-guessing myself, I hurried after him. He was walking down the hallway and he seemed like he was in a hurry. I caught up to him and he didn't say a word to me.

"Hey," I said trying to catch my breath. "I want to know what's going on."

"I'm not in the mood today."

What the hell was that supposed to mean? He was never in the mood for anything unless it was on his terms. I've had enough of just sitting around waiting for answers. He was going to tell me what was going on because I deserved that much. I grabbed his arm forcing him to stop.

He yanked his arm away, "I told you that I'm not in the mood."

"What's wrong with you? Why are you acting like this? It's like you're so distant. Is there something going on? Did I do something to you? I don't understand why you're being like this."

"Why do you give a fuck anyway? You're here to save your brother and that's the only thing that you need to be worried about. I play with you when I feel like it and today I'm not in the fucking mood. Go to your room and stay out of my way."

I was growing more and more angrier by the second. "What will you do if I don't?" I knew that I shouldn't challenge him but I couldn't help it.

He stepped towards me but I held my ground. "Don't be stupid, Aya. It wouldn't be smart of you to challenge me when I'm in a bad mood."

I threw my hands in the air. "Why are you in a bad mood? Is it because you didn't get to murder that guy back there? Why are you always trying to punish everybody around you. It's like you live to punish people. You get off on hurting people and I don't understand why. You wanted to kill him and now you're upset because you can't."

He shoved me against the wall. "I can do whatever the fuck I want. If I want to go and kill him, I'll go kill him right now. Stop acting like you know me when you don't. I haven't shown you half of what I'm capable of."

"But why? Why do you have to be so ruthless? It doesn't make sense to me, and I want you to explain it to me."

"I don't have to explain anything to you. You are here for me to play with and nothing more. I don't owe you a damn thing, and me sparing your brother is saying a lot because I don't give second chances."

"I feel like you want to punish me. Instead of punishing my brother and that guy back there, you want to punish me and you're frustrated because you can't. It's not me that you want to punish, it's Athena. You want to punish anyone who looks like her."

He stared at me for a second, "you think you know everything. You don't know anything about me and what I want."

"You love her," I whispered.

"My life doesn't revolve around Athena. I don't know how many times I have to tell you that. She is nothing to me and she will never be. Stop bringing her name up because the next time you do, I'll make you fucking regret it."

I knew that despite what he said, he loved her. There was something dark brewing inside Vain and I knew that any day he would lose it. I knew that he would snap one day, and I feared him hurting an innocent person. He walked away leaving me standing there alone. It wasn't my job to fix him and I didn't want to. But I had to protect myself and my brother. Vain was like a ticking time bomb. If he couldn't get his emotions under control, he would end up killing my brother. I had this feeling in the pit of my stomach and it scared me.

I hope you all enjoyed this chapter

BASKETBALL

I decided not to question Vain any more than what I had. I knew that he wasn't in the mood and I didn't want to test his patience any further than I did yesterday. I was shocked when he told me that we would be playing a game today. I thought that given his bad mood, we would take a break but I was mistaken. He told me to meet him at the basketball court in his back yard. I hoped that today wouldn't be like yesterday. I wasn't in the mood to see anyone get hurt. I was over being in control of someone else's fate. As I walked to the basketball court, I could see him in the distance.

He was standing there shirtless with a pair of black sweatpants hanging low on his hips. The sun was shining on his skin and I could see his tattoos clearly. He was a sight for the eyes but I knew what type of man he was. The closer that I got to him, the more my heart seem to beat faster. I wasn't ready for what he was going to make me do. He turned around to face me and smiled. He was holding a basketball and I waited patiently for him to explain what we were going to do. From what I could see, it seemed like he was in a better mood.

"So, have you ever played basketball before?"

"I played but it wasn't anything serious."

He smiled, "good. I would hate to have to go over the rules of basketball with you. As long as you know the basics, you will be fine. Today, we are going to be playing a simple game of basketball. Whoever makes it to ten points first wins the game. Since you won the last game, I'll let you go first."

He threw the ball at me and I caught it. He didn't strike me as the type of man that would enjoy to play basketball, but he continued to surprise me. I was grateful that this was a simple game of basketball and nothing more. I wasn't any good at basketball but I was hoping that maybe he wasn't either. I dribbled the ball towards the center of the court and he watched from a distance. I bounced the ball up and down before finally grasping it in my hands and throwing it towards the goal. The ball hit the rim and bounced off. It wasn't a good shot and so I wasn't disappointed. I ran after the ball so that I could pass it to him. Before the ball could get too far away from me, I grabbed it, and headed back towards him. I threw it at him, and he caught it with ease.

"I hope you know that this is like a real game of basketball. We are not going to sit here and take turns making shots. You are going to have to play and try to take the ball for me."

"Okay," I whispered. I played basketball a few times throughout my life but it wasn't anything major. I knew the basics of basketball because my father used to watch it but I never paid attention. I knew that I had to do the best that I could, and that's what I planned on doing. He took off running towards the goal and I chased after him. He was much faster than I was, and before I could stop him, he threw the ball towards the goal. The ball rolled around the rim before finally falling in.

He laughed, "that's three points for me."

Three points? How did he get three points so fast?

"When you make a shot from the center of the court, that's three points."

I was glad that he took time to explain that to me. But if he kept making shots from where he was, he would reach ten points in no time. If I couldn't defend the ball and he took it from me, this would be an easy win for him. He went and got the ball and tossed it to me. I caught it and took off running towards the goal quickly. I knew that I couldn't make a shot from the center of the court, and so I decided not to risk it. If I got closer to the goal, I would have a better chance. He was right behind me, and as I jumped to make my shot, he knocked the ball out of my hand.

"You have to have a better defense than that, Aya."

I rolled my eyes and placed my hand on my hip. This wasn't going to be a game I was going to be able to win.

As I suspected, I didn't win the game. He beat me easily, but I already seen that coming so I wasn't shocked. We were even now; I had won two games, and so did he. We had six more games to play, and I had to win the majority of them. His mood swings changed like the seasons, and I never knew when it was a good time for him. There were times where I felt like he was patient and understanding, but then there were times where he didn't care. Despite his mood swings, he was in charge. He was starting to play games that he favored, and I knew that it was going to be my downfall. I had no choice but to try to up my game so that I could beat him and save my brother.

"Good game, but you need more practice."

I shrugged, "you don't strike me as a basketball player.":

"I used to play when I was a kid."

"Why did you stop?"

He ran his fingers through his hair, "my duty to my family took over."

I watched as the sweat ran down his body and I bit my lip. "There has to be more to you than just your duty to your family. Don't you have hobbies other than playing mafia?" I was curious to know more about him because I felt like there was more to him than what he allowed people to see.

He smirked, "I don't play Mafia. I am the mafia and people fear me. I don't have any hobbies at all because most of them died when I was younger. The only thing that I care about now is making sure that I run the family the way that I should. Family is everything and you should know that."

"Yeah, that's true. But what is the point of family if you're going to be miserable in the end?" I loved how devoted he was his family but it only made him bitter. "I don't know much about it, but I feel like there should be things that you get to enjoy. It's great that you live for your family, and your devotion is very strong, but make sure you put yourself first. Have you ever heard the term that self-love is the best love."

"I enjoy doing this and it is one of my hobbies. This is my life, and I've learned to live with it."

"So, you don't have any other hobbies other than this one? You don't like to do anything else besides run the family? I don't believe that at all."

"Believe what you want, Aya. The thing is...basketball was more fun when I had friends. I had one friend that I used to play with and he used to beat me every time. We only got to play a few times before my father finally told me that I couldn't play with him anymore. So, my passion for basketball is no longer there. I don't like doing anything else, but maybe I would if I had the chance to experience new things."

"But you can experience new things if you want to. There is so much to do in the city. You live in New York and you have endless resources at your feet. Take a vacation and sight see. Travel the world and learn more about yourself. That's what my parents always told me. They told me that life is too short to be miserable, and we should find what we love and do it."

He tossed me the ball and I caught it. "I wish it was that easy, Aya. It must be fun being able to decide your own fate. You wouldn't understand because your life wasn't chosen for you. You get to do whatever you want to do. You get to choose who you want to love and who you want to marry. I don't have that and I never did. My family is the strictest family out of the four mafia families. Any of the interest that I had were all taken from me because they were not important. The most important thing is my family, and I learned that at a very early age. Besides, when my parents come to visit they never stay long. My father treats it as though it's an audit. I never feel like he wants to visit me and catch up on what's been going on. Most of the time, he always tells me what I am doing wrong, and how to fix it."

"That sounds awful," I whispered. "How about your mother?"

"She hates New York, so she doesn't come. I have to visit her in Spain, and we spend time together but it's rare."

I hated to hear that he didn't get to spend much time with his mother. Maybe that was why he was the way that he was. "I see." That's all I could say because I didn't want to upset him. It seemed like talking about his parents put him in a bad mood. I watched the sun set in the distance. It was a beautiful sight and it was peaceful. Being here with him like this was nice. "It's so beautiful," I smiled.

"How do you do that?" He asked turning away from me.

"Do what?"

"You always find a way to smile even though you shouldn't. What makes you happy, Aya. What are some of your interests?"

I rubbed the back of my neck nervously, "well, I love reading. I enjoy painting, and I going to look at artwork. I was starting my photography business, but I...well here I am because of my brother."

"Do you hate him?"

His question took me by surprise. Why would I hate Aito? "Um...no...I mean he gets on my nerves, but that's what big brothers do. All that we have is each other, and despite the small fights that we have, I love him. Sometimes you have to forgive people even when you don't want to. It helps you because you're not carrying around all that hate and anger."

"I don't have that capability, and I never did. The man that I hate is still alive and I can't forgive him. That's why I tortured him for so long. I won't stop until I take away everything that he loves, then I will be happy to move on."

My eyes widened and I dropped the ball. Before I could respond, he walked away leaving me alone. In a weird way I felt bad for him because I felt like his whole life was being controlled. But he was right, I knew nothing about it. I had a will of my own and I wasn't raised in a strict family that controlled everything that I did. It wasn't easy for him and it still isn't because his dedication to his family will never leave him. But I hated to see that it was making him bitter and angry. Because his family took away any potential interest that he had, being this way is all that he knew. It's like his family groomed him to be this way, and that sucked for everyone around him, and the people that he encountered.

I hope you all enjoyed this chapter

SATONI

Book #1 of the Tainted IV Series. Add to your library now !!

DAY OF REST

V AIN POV

    We played two more games and Aya was fortunate enough to win them. I think I was to the point where I didn't care. They were simple games and I decided to let her win. Today, I just wanted to relax. I needed a day to ease my mind and stop thinking of all the pressure and stress in my life. My father was pushing me to seal the deal with the Russian mafia, and I didn't have it in me to talk to them. They were idiots, and I didn't understand why my father wanted to do business with them. We had endless money at our feet, and we didn't need to get involved with another country. I decided that I would go meet with them at the end of the week. It would be better for me anyway because I wouldn't be so tense. I felt like I was a ticking time bomb and I didn't understand why. It seemed like everything and everyone was starting to piss me off. I've been so busy with running my family and playing these little games with Aya that I didn't even realize that I hadn't had sex. That could be a reason why I was so tense. I pulled my phone out and sent one of my whore's a text. She meant nothing to me and I always paid her after. I looked down when my phone buzzed. She said that she would be here in 10 minutes and sent me a couple of heart emoji's. I was desperate to relieve the stress that was building inside of me. Maybe while she was here, I could take some of my frustration out on her. My phone started to ring and I looked down. Great, my father was calling me. I answered on the third ring and waited for him to speak.

"What happened to the deal with Russia?"

"I'm still going to go. But I need a day to myself because I have been working nonstop. If I go to that meeting today, I'll lose my shit and you know it. I'm not in the mood to sit around and talk to them. They don't speak my language and they have. I've met with them two times and they keep saying the same thing. Our money works differently than theirs."

He sighed, "what has so worked up? You haven't been the same these days and I want to know what's going on. Your mind should be on business, but it's not. Do you care to enlighten me on what could be more important to sealing the deal with Russia?"

"If you want the deal in Russia, you go to the meeting. I told you that I've had enough and I need a day to myself. If you have anything else that you want me to do, I'll be more than happy. But putting me in a setting like that will only cause me to shoot someone."

"Okay listen, I understand. You're not a machine and I need to stop treating you like one. If you need a few days to yourself, you can take off and I'll have my men fill-in."

"Thanks," I mumbled.

"I need you here one hundred percent, so I need you to tell me what's bothering you. I know that you are not entitled to tell me anything but you are my son, and I care about your well-being."

"I'm just dealing with a lot, that's all. But you don't have to worry, I'll be sure to balance everything. If you need me, just give me a call."

He said OK and ended the call quickly. That was one thing about my father that I hated the most. He was stubborn but that was because he was old and set in his ways. When he wanted things done, he wanted them done. He didn't care that you were tired or you had something else to do. I wanted him to understand that I was his son and not one of his soldiers. I think that it's because he's old that he fears leaving everything to me. He told me that once and I couldn't argue with him. Running New York was challenging and it kept me busy. That's what Athena didn't understand. She didn't understand that I was a busy man and my life never stopped. I wanted to be the man that she wanted me to be. I wanted to be the husband and father but I couldn't. When I was a kid, my father would leave me alone with my mother all the time. I would barely see him until he started to groom me for the mafia. I would be with my mother for weeks at a time without seeing my father. That's not the way that I wanted to raise my kid and I wouldn't. Not only that but losing the love of my life showed me a lot of things. There would always be an enemy lurking in the shadows ready to take away the one thing that makes you happy. There was a soft knock at my door and I smirked, she was here. I stood up and walked over to my bedroom door quickly. I pulled the door open to see Azira standing there in a red lace bra with matching panties. She didn't wait for me to give her permission to walk into my bedroom. She walked past me and bent over the bed. That's what I loved most about her. She knew what I liked, and she wasn't shy like the others. I didn't have to walk her through every step of pleasing me. She did with no hesitation, and that thought alone caused my cock to grow very hard. I walked over to her and spanked her hard, and she gasped. I was going to have fun with her, and hopefully relieve some of my stress.

"Are you ready to please me?"

She licked her lips slowly, "yes. I am yours to do what you want with. There is no greater pleasure than pleasing a man like you."

I smirked, "get down on your knees, now."

She got down and started to undo my belt and I watched her eagerly. She was going to spend some time worshipping me like she promised.

After an hour and a half, I felt like I was finally satisfied and so I sent Azira on her way. I laid in bed staring up at the ceiling deep in thought. No matter how many times I tried to tell myself not to think about Athena, I always did. I couldn't understand what it was about her except for the fact that I wanted to torture Satoni. I kept trying to tell myself that I never really truly loved her, but would that be a lie? I closed my eyes and laid there listening to the soft tick of the clock that was on the wall across the room. I was tired and after being up for the past two days, I was going to sleep.

I watched as my mom packed her things. She had enough of my father cheating on her. She didn't like America because she felt like she didn't belong. She had a hard time learning English, and it was miserable for her. My father would keep her locked up in the house all the time. She started to feel like a prisoner. I watched as he came to her and tried to embrace her from behind. She pushed him away and walked over to the closet. I was sitting there scrolling on my phone quietly. It was their argument to work out and I didn't want to get involved.

"I'm sick of this. I'm tired of being trapped in this house like this. I am not an object; you can't do this." My mother yelled in Italian.

"I do all of this to keep you safe," my father replied.

"Shove your excuses down your throat, okay? You don't do this to keep me safe! You do this because you want to have control over me. You like the title of having a wife because I make you look like a good person. But I will not continue to do this with you. I'm going back to Spain, and you can have the whores and money you constantly chase."

He grabbed her arm, "you are my family, Livia."

She laughed and yanked her arm free. "Family? You think that we are family? You have no idea how to treat your family. You married me because I got pregnant. You trapped me and you know it, Victor. We dated for six months and I told you I was leaving you and next thing I know, I'm pregnant. You want everything your way, and it doesn't work like that. You will not have the luxury of having multiple women and then you come home to me after you laid next to another woman."

He sighed running his fingers through his hair. "It was a mistake, and you know it."

"That was girl number twelve. Please stop with your bullshit excuses. They are making me sick to my stomach. I am taking Vain with me. He doesn't need to be around you and all of your many whores."

"You are not taking him away from me. He has things that he needs to learn and he won't learn them from being with you. You can't teach him how to run the family, Livia. If you want to have a tantrum, go ahead. I'll let you have the house in Spain. But Vain stays with me so that I can teach him everything that he needs to know."

She rolled her eyes, "teach him what? All you want to teach him is how to use women. He needs to see a different side of how to treat women. You control every part of his life, including who he talks to. You can't do that, Victor. You have to let him build his own social skills. He will never know what it's like to be a good man. I want different for him and you should too."

"Trust me, I'll teach him."

"How?" She asked throwing her hands in the air. "The only thing you teach him how to do is sleep around and cheat. You don't know what it's like to be devoted to one person. Oh, yea you do actually. You are devoted to Sergio Patel and he used to beat his wife. We still don't know what happened to Ana. You choose them over your family and so I'm choosing my happiness over you. I will take my son with me, and we will go back to Spain."

He grabbed her arm roughly, "Livia, don't do this. He is my son, and the heir to everything we own. If I don't set him up for success, he will be killed. He is my son and he needs to know how to hold his own. I won't be here forever and neither will you."

"That's why it's important that we teach him correctly before it's too late. He is fourteen, Victor. He will be eighteen in four years. I don't want to be the mother of a heart breaker. I don't want him to grow up thinking that it's okay to mistreat women. If you want to set a good example for him, start doing better yourself. Treat me the way that I'm supposed to be treated by you. I am your wife and you made a vow to me. You are breaking every single promise that you made to me."

He kissed her hand, "I'm sorry."

"Sorry won't keep me here. I'm leaving and I'll be back to check on Vain. You need to start being devoted to him. He is the only son that you have, and you will regret it if you don't build a bond with him." Those were the last words that she said before she walked out of the bedroom leaving me alone with my father. She was right back then, but nothing ever changed.

I hope you all enjoyed this chapter

VICTOR GREY

Today Vain was taking me to see Aito and I was surprised but excited. I wanted to see my brother more than anything because I needed to make sure that he was okay. We walked inside a nice house that was located in Manhattan. I was shocked by the luxurious life that he lived. He had money, power, and status. All of the men that were guarding the house made sure to greet him correctly. They would call him Don or say something quick in Italian. We walked into the backyard and I was happy to see Aito standing there. He was standing beside two men with guns and I knew instantly that we couldn't try anything funny. I didn't waste anytime running into his arms. He embraced me tightly and I couldn't stop myself from crying. He rubbed my back and told me that everything was okay and that he was okay. I pulled away and stared into his eyes.

I knew Korean and so I decided to talk in our native tongue to help us talk amongst ourselves. "How are you?" I asked quickly.

"I'm okay," he sighed. "How is everything going with the games?"

"It's going, I'm in the lead right now."

Vain cleared his throat and I turned around to face him. "Speak English, I don't like it when I can't understand you."

I ran my fingers through my hair and cursed under my breath. "If that's what you want."

He took a step towards me, "lose the attitude."

I sighed and turned back to face my brother. "I'm glad that you're okay. I have missed you so much but I want to kill you at the same time. What the hell were you thinking getting mixed up with men like this? You weren't thinking about me, you were thinking about yourself."

He looked down at his feet for a second. "I know, Aya. I should have been honest with you, but I couldn't. I didn't want you to know about this part of my life."

I frowned, "this isn't a part of our lives. We don't have any ties to these people and you shouldn't have dealt with them. They can't be trusted, you know that. Mom and dad made sure that we never saw things like this. Do you have any idea what I've been through and what I've seen?"

He grabbed my hand and squeezed it, "I'm sorry. I was an idiot to get mixed up in all of this and I regret it. I should have never did any of it and I'm sorry. But we will get out of this and I promise we can go wherever you want and I'll be a better brother for you."

I wanted to be angry with him, but I couldn't. He was my brother and I loved him even though he was stupid at times. I squeezed his hand back and smiled weakly. "I'm going to hold you to that."

"Vain, I'm glad to see that you are back on your feet."

Vain's eyes widened and I frowned when I noticed a man walking towards us. It was weird because he looked very similar to Vain. His dark brown hair was gelled back just like Vain's and it was still nice even with the grey streaks in it. He had the same grey eyes that made you feel as though they were looking right into your soul. He was just about as tall as Vain. I could tell that Vain was not happy about this man being here and I couldn't help but wonder why.

VAIN

My father wasn't supposed to be here today. I told him that I wasn't in the mood for his bullshit and he flew all the way here from Texas to piss me off. Now was not the time to lecture me about the man I killed the other day. I've been on edge these days and he can tell, but it wasn't his business. He walked up to me and placed his hand on my shoulder. I greeted him in Italian and he smirked.

"You look alert today," He said in Italian.

I sighed, "I'm doing much better than I was yesterday."

He gripped my shoulder tightly, "why the hell did you think it was okay to kill Oscar? I sent him to give you a message and you killed him. He was one of my best men, Vain."

I stared into his eyes, "I told him to come back later and he didn't. I won't be disrespected by anyone, and that includes your men."

He chuckled, "I see. We have much to discuss, son. So, let's go have this conversation over some lunch." He looked over slowly and his eyes widened when he saw Aya standing there with Aito. I knew that he wasn't going to be happy about seeing them here.

"Old habits die hard I see."

I bit my lip and stepped aside, "I have business with them." He didn't need to know anything else.

"She looks just like your lover, Athena." He smiled at her and she took a step back. The last thing I wanted was for him to mention Athena around her.

"Athena was sexier," I shrugged.

He laughed and patted me on the back quickly. "Now I see where all your frustration is coming from. What is your name?" He asked turning to look at Aya. She was scared, that was a good thing. At least she would be on her best behavior. I didn't want her embarrassing me in front of my father, but her very presence was doing that already.

"Aya...Aya Varloni and this is my brother Aito."

He raised an eyebrow, "are you Italian?"

"We are mixed. Half Italian, that comes from my father. Half Korean, that comes from my mother."

He stared at her for a second before laughing. "You found another tainted woman. It's weird that she is mixed with the same exact thing as Athena."

I wasn't in the mood to be mocked, "she has one purpose here. She is here to clear a debt and that's all. I have no interest in fucking her or loving her. Now, we have much to discuss. I started to walk away and he followed me. I wanted to keep things short and sweet. The less he knew the better, but I wasn't hiding anything either. I wanted nothing to do with Aya sexually. We walked into the dining room and I took a seat at the table. He sat across from me and I waited for him to speak.

"There are rules in the mafia and you have to follow them. You are being consumed with women and fun that you are blind to your destiny."

"What destiny is that?" I asked unbuttoning the top button of my shirt.

"You are here to run the family and help get us to the number one spot. We are third and we will always be third if we don't surpass the Romano family."

Ever since I was little that is all that he talked about. He didn't like that we were number three within the four ranks. He felt like we should be number one because we didn't taint our bloodline. But what he failed to realize is that we originated in Spain. The Romano family and Patel family originated in Italy. They were the two families who started all of this and took Italy first.

"You know that will never be possible. They took over the Italian mafia before we could. There is no changing that. We originated in Spain, so we are the outsiders and it doesn't matter that we are Italian. We are the filthy blood in the Mafia. Even the Vintalli family originated in Italy. They have all the rights there, not us."

"The Vintalli family was put on the pedestal that they have. They shouldn't even be a part of the four ranks."

"Why? Because they were helped by the Romano family? It doesn't matter if they had help or not, they originated there. So, we can't go in and take over the Italian mafia when it isn't ours to take. Besides, we originated after the Patel family, so there is nothing that we can do to change that. Yes, we might have more money and power, but ranks can't be changed. I don't care about the ranks anyway. As long as we are taking care of our family and making money why should I care?"

He sighed, "it's about so much more than that. That's why I'm trying to get the Russian Mafia on our side."

I sat up slowly, "what do you mean?"

"With their resources, we can make so much happen. We can take California business from Satoni."

"That's not your decision to make. If I want to destroy Satoni that is my choice to make. When you gave me New York, you told me that I run things in this country. You have no say so here and you know it. Stop trying to overstep your boundaries."

He held his hand up in surrender, "you're right. I can't make the rules over here. But you are my son and I can guide you. I want you to be smart about everything that's going on. You lost the woman that you love to him. The woman that you finally opened your heart to chose him over you. Do you want to continue to let them win and take everything that is meant for us...that is meant for you."

I was pissed that Athena was given to Satoni, but what could I do? I didn't love her anyway, so it didn't matter. "I don't love her and you know that. Even if I did, I wouldn't be able to marry her. She was not fully Italian and that would be a dishonor." My father was here to get inside my head and I wouldn't let him.

"You want to keep the peace and I know that, but we didn't start the war. Satoni did when he killed your soon to be wife. I'm not here to tell you what to do, but you are becoming weak. You are Vain Grey and it's time that you got your revenge. He has Athena and you can kill her. Make him feel what you felt when you lost the woman that you loved."

I smirked, "this is why you wanted Athena to go back to him. You wanted him to have the life that I was having. Now, you want me to take it away."

He stood up, "yes. He took my first grandchild from me, and now I want him to know true pain."

"I already did, I tainted his bride. He will never have the luxury of being her first. He has to live with the fact that I will forever be her first. He will never take that title away from me. I have nothing more that I want to do to him or Athena. That part of my life is over and you know that. Now, if we are done here, I have something that I have to do." I stood up quickly and tried to walk past him, but he stopped me.

He grabbed my arm, "you say that, but we both know the truth. Are you in therapy because of Isabella or Athena. Which one can't you get over? Because I'm pretty sure it's not Isabella."

I snatched my arm away from him, "why do you care? If you cared about me, you would have let me marry Athena."

"You didn't want to marry her, Vain. You wanted to fuck her and you did. You were infatuated with her and you still are and now it's time to let it go. Kill the little bitch and get it over with. You will be even with Satoni and you will be satisfied."

"Are you forgetting that Roman will come after us?"

He laughed, "with what resources? The ones that Satoni is giving to him. Their family is in poverty, everyone knows it. If you take away his bride, that will weaken him more than you know." He patted me on the back before leaving me standing there alone.

I hope you all enjoyed this chapter

HEARTLESS

Today I was supposed to be meeting with my therapist again and I was growing tired of these sessions. They never helped me uncover how I truly felt and now I was feeling like it was a waste of my time. But I decided to give this one last try before I finally told my therapist that I was done with these meaningless sessions. She walked into the room and smiled at me before taking a seat in her usual chair. I laid on the couch, kicked my feet up, and closed my eyes. If I was going to do this, I had to be relaxed.

"So, I just want to jump right into things. I have been your therapist for a while and I feel like we still haven't uncovered the answers that you seek. So, today I'm going to take a different approach and hopefully we can get down to the bottom of why you feel the way that you do."

I agreed because she was a therapist not me. Besides, I was curious about this new approach that she was deciding to take. But before we could get started I needed to tell her about the conversation that I had with my father earlier.

"Before we start I need to tell you something. My father feels like I should kill Athena. He feels like if I do, I will no longer be infatuated with her. But I don't even feel like it's an infatuation."

She smiled weakly, "you seem a little confused. I want to help you and that's why I'm here. So, before we get into all of that I want to just recap on everything that we've covered since I've been your therapist." She bought out her clipboard and sat up straight. "You said that there was no abuse in your home between your parents, is that correct?"

"Yes."

"You said that growing up you were always trying to make your father proud. You didn't want to do anything that would displease him."

"Yes, that's correct."

"Do you think that going above and beyond to please your father has made you bitter? Because it seems like to me that you have missed out on a lot of opportunities, and things that you want to do because your father would not approve of it."

I thought about it for a second before responding. "Yeah, but I always felt like my father had my best interest so I never questioned him."

She took a second to write something down on her clipboard before continuing. "You said that your mother was always very loving and supportive of anything that you chose to do. You also said that you love your mother."

"Yes, I love my mother very much. She has always been very supportive of anything that I wanted to do and always encouraged me to fall in love and settle down."

"Your childhood was lonely but it wasn't as bad as it could have been."

I opened my eyes and stared up at the ceiling. "Yes, my childhood was very lonely but it wasn't filled with abuse. I was sheltered as a child because my parents wanted to protect me. So, there was a lot of things that I didn't see."

"As soon as you were able to date you did. You met a young woman named Isabella and you fell in love. You wanted to marry her and you didn't see yourself loving anyone else. But you met Athena before you met her. Did you have any type of feelings towards Athena at all?"

"No, my father never allowed me to play with Roman again so there wasn't much to know about Athena. I had no feelings towards her at all because I didn't know her."

She wrote something down on her clipboard and smiled at me. "Now, let's talk about Satoni. What was your relationship like with Satoni?"

"I got to spend a little bit of time with him because we were both Italian from what I knew. I didn't know that he had cousins that were of mixed blood. But he is full Italian and we got along well. I was ten when I met him for the first time."

"Now, I want you to close your eyes and think about that memory. Go back to that place and tell me how you felt."

I closed my eyes and relaxed trying to take myself back to the day that I met Satoni for the first time.

I watched as a young boy about my age aimed the gun at the target and pulled the trigger. The bullet hit the mannequin right in the forehead. I couldn't help but feel amazed at his aim. I wasn't as good as him but I was getting there. He looked over at me and smiled and I smiled back.

"Hey, I didn't even notice you there. My father must be having another business meeting."

"Yeah, my dad is here too. I'm Vain Grey and it's nice to meet you."

He sat the gun down and grabbed my hand shaking it. "It's a pleasure to meet you. My name is Satoni Romano. Do you come to these often?"

My eyes widened; he was the son of Emilio Romano. They are ranked number one within the four mafia families. I didn't want to seem so surprised so I tried to remain calm and collected. "I try not to. They're boring and a waste of my time."

He laughed, "I'm glad to know that someone feels the same way that I do. When I told my father that, he had a heart attack. I try not to mention it anymore because he'll usually give me a two-hour long lecture about the importance of these meetings. Anyway, do you want to shoot some Bow and arrows with me?"

My eyes widened again, "that sounds cool."

I followed him as we made our way to the other side of the field. His backyard was full of all kinds of cool things to do. He had archery, a track field, a gun range, a basketball court, and so much more. He handed me a bow and I took it. He grabbed one and then handed me an arrow, and I waited patiently for him to shoot first. I've never done archery before so I wasn't sure how to do it. The bow was heavy, and the arrow was sharp from what I could see.

"So, how do you feel about the Vintalli family?"

The question took me by surprise and I wasn't sure how to answer it. Why was he asking about the Vintalli family? "They seem pretty cool. I played basketball with Roman once a few years ago. But I haven't seen them since and I don't know what they're up to. Why do you ask?"

He shrugged and aimed his arrow at the target before pulling the string back and letting it go. The arrow shot forward and hit the colorful board across the field right in the center. "I was just curious because my father has taken an interest in them. I've been around Roman and he's very quiet but he's good at archery. You should come over sometime and we can all play together."

I stared down at my feet nervously, "I would like to but my father said that I'm not allowed to play with tainted blood."

He turned to look at me and frowned, "tainted blood? What do you mean by that?"

"My father said that I'm not allowed to play with anyone that's not fully Italian."

He raised an eyebrow, "that's odd. My father said that it's important that we all get along. He says that once they all die off we are all that we have. If I can make friends out of all of you, I would like to. Having enemies is too much work."

I opened my eyes and smirked, "it was nice. Meeting Satoni for the first time was very nice, and he seemed like a good leader."

"I'm glad to hear that. So, let's skip ahead, you start to date his sister. Things don't work out and you end up breaking up with her, and then falling in love with Isabella. Be honest with me, did you ever cheat on his sister with Isabella?"

I sighed, "I'm not going to sit here and pretend that I'm perfect. I'm a man and sometimes men make mistakes. I wasn't perfect in the relationship and I did cheat on her but she wasn't perfect either. I wanted to be with Isabella and I had every right to move on. It's not my fault that his sister was suicidal and couldn't handle the truth."

"What disappointed you about that situation the most? I feel like you have this hidden hatred for Satoni and it's not just about Athena."

"What disappointed me about that situation the most was the fact that Satoni didn't even hear me out. He assumed that I was the reason for his sister's death and it hurt me because I thought that we were friends. He was a leader that I looked up to and that leader let me down. He jumped to conclusions and killed someone that I loved. He didn't just kill her, but he also killed my legacy. He killed my unborn child, and I will never forgive him for that."

"So, you felt like by being the leader that he should look at all the evidence in front of him. You feel like he voted in favor of his sister and ignored your feelings and your explanation."

"Yes."

She started to write on her clipboard again and things were quiet for a second. "So, it was your father's idea for you to taint Athena. He felt like if you took his bride things would be even. Is that something that you wanted to do?"

"I didn't want to hurt Athena but I felt like I had to make a statement. Years had passed and Satoni thought that things were okay between us. I wanted him to know that I would never forget what he did, and I would continue to get my revenge until I felt like it was enough. Even though I knew that Athena was innocent in all of this, I couldn't stop thinking about the fact that Isabella was too. Isabella died because she loved me and that is the only crime that she ever committed."

"The truth is, you've been watching over Athena ever since she was little. Even when your father wanted you to do a stakeout, and you realized that Athena was there. You changed your mind because she was there, and you didn't want to hurt her and kill her father and her brother in front of her."

"I'm not a monster. I don't get off on hurting innocent people."

"I'm glad to know that, Vain. I think that you are a very caring person and I feel like you have cared from the very beginning. You aim to please your father, and because you want to please him and make him proud, you hurt other people." She sighed, "do you think that maybe your father had something to do with the death of Satoni's sister?"

I frowned, "no. Why would you think that?"

"Your father is always pushing you to be the replica of him. But he also wants to be number one within the mafia ranks. Do you think that maybe he played a part in her death so that he could start a war? He wanted to make them weak and that was the way to do it. He wants to destroy the Romano family. So, could it be possible?"

"I don't know. My father has been known to do some very outrageous things."

"Maybe it's worth looking into. I'm not here to tell you what to do because I can't. But what I would suggest is to learn to ask the right questions and to heal from the past. You can't change what happened. Innocent women were killed because of the war between the two of you. No one else needs to get hurt and you know that. It's time to put your pride to the side and move on. Your father will keep dictating your life if he knows that he can. He told you that he wanted you to take Athena's virginity and that would even the score. But now here he is again making demands and asking you to kill an innocent woman so that he can have what he wants. The question here is, what do you want?"

I've never thought about it before or asked myself that question. What did I want? That was a very difficult question that I had no answer to. I wanted to be happy and move on from the past but it seemed like the past just kept haunting me. I wanted to let go of Isabella and everything that happened, but I couldn't. I knew that there was this darkness in me. It would probably always be there and no one could fix it.

"Maybe I'm just fucked up. Maybe I just have no idea who the hell I am. Maybe I want to use women. Maybe I was bored, and I used Athena to keep me entertained."

"Maybe you fear falling in love again because you don't want to lose the person you love. You loved Athena. You might not have loved her as a lover but you loved her as a friend and a person. And you lost her to the very man that you lost Isabella to. You couldn't stand the thought that Athena was to be married to the very man that took away the woman that you loved. You wanted to torture her even though you knew it wasn't her fault. You knew that she knew nothing of her marriage with Satoni but it angered you anyway. You don't want to lose anyone else that you love. But it is also important that you remember that you don't want to miss the opportunity to tell the people that you love that you do love them. I wasn't there and I don't know the pain of losing a lover especially so gruesome. But I feel like you would feel so much better if you just admitted how you truly felt. You are a person and you have feelings. You are not one of your fathers' soldiers that he can command. So, right here and right now I want you to tell me how you really feel."

"I feel like this is a bunch of bullshit. I hate these therapy sessions and I hate opening up to people. Nobody understands what the fuck I've been through, but everybody tries. Why is it so hard to understand that I don't love anyone? The last person I loved was taken from me and I will never love again. Athena was my revenge and that is all that she will ever be. I do not love her and I will never love her."

"You don't love her because she is tainted blood?"

"I don't love her because I can't love her. Isabella took my heart with her when she died. So, there was nothing left when I met Athena."

She shook her head, "So, you are missing your heart. It's your choice to get it back, Vain. You don't have to be like this?"

"Trust me, I'm better off without it," I mumbled.

She took a deep breath, "okay. You have completed your therapy sessions and there is nothing more that can be done. I have asked all the right questions and you have given me all the answers. Whatever you choose to do going forward is completely up to you. If you don't love Athena, I can't make you. If she was just something for you to use, that was completely your decision. Isabella is your first love and your forever love. She will forever have your heart even in death. Good bye, Mr. Grey. It's been a pleasure."

She picked up her briefcase and took one last look at me before leaving me alone in the room. This was it, no more therapy sessions. There was nobody in the world that could help me understand why I was better off without my heart. This darkness that lingered inside of me would always be there, and there was nothing that I could do about it.

I hope you all enjoyed this chapter

DREAM OR REALITY

V ain and I played two more games and I was lucky enough to win them both. We only had two more games left and as of right now I was in the lead. I was happy that I was winning but at the same time it bothered me because I knew that he wasn't in the right mindset. I felt like he didn't even care about the games anymore and was allowing me to win at this point. I wanted to talk to him about allowing me to leave now. I walked into the pool room and he was playing pool by himself. I hadn't seen him all day but I had a feeling that he was going to be here. When he saw me enter the room he looked up and went right back to playing pool.

"I was wondering if we could talk."

"About what?" He mumbled hitting the ball into the hole.

"I know that you have had a lot going on lately and I feel like you don't care about the games as much anymore. I am winning right now and we only have two more games to play, and I just feel like we shouldn't play them. I can tell that you are no longer interested and you're letting me win."

He laid the stick down on the table and took a step towards me. "Is that what you think?"

I was hesitant to answer but I knew that's why I came. I came to talk to him so that we could get a better understanding of what was truly going on. "Yes, that's what I think and I'll be more than happy to leave and take my brother with me."

"It doesn't matter if you are in the lead. You still have to play ten games and don't think for a second that I'm allowing you to win."

"There's no point in us playing anymore. I've won six games and you've only won two. Even if you were to win the last two games I would still be the winner. There's no point in fighting a losing battle."

I blinked and he was standing right in front of me. He was fast and now he was upset. I could tell by the look in his eyes. "It doesn't matter if you've won. I am the one that makes the decisions and if I want to kill your brother, I will."

"You are so heartless. I don't know what your problem is and it's not my job to figure it out. You can't go back on what you said. I won so release my brother and give me my one million. At this point, I don't even care about the money. I just want to take my brother and leave this place."

He smirked, "you think that you have it all figured out. Don't be stupid, Aya. I decide your fate, and it would be wise if you didn't piss me off."

"You have no right to say that. You do not decide my fate and I wouldn't be here if it wasn't for my brother. I don't know what you have going on but that's completely up to you to fix. You've been in a bad mood for three weeks and I'm over it. I am over being forced to be here and stay here when I don't want to. I want to be able to go back to college and do everything that I was doing before you came into my life and interrupted it."

He grabbed me by the arm and yanked me towards him. "Do you really want to put your little theory to the test? I make the rules and I can change them whenever I want to. If I want you to fuck me, you will. You will do whatever I ask you to do to save your brother."

I stared at him in disgust, "you're disgusting. I would never give myself to you and I'm pretty sure that we already had this conversation. There is nothing more that we need to talk about. I won the games and I'm going to get my brother so that we can go home."

I tried to get away from him but he pulled me closer. "You're not going anywhere." Before I could stop him he lifted me onto the pool table and spread my legs. I struggled against him but he was much stronger than me. I had no idea what he was going to do and that scared me. "You've been tempting me for a while now and I'm ready to take what you really want to give me."

"Don't be stupid, you're the last man that I would ever give myself to. I'm not like Athena or your ex-Isabella. They fell in love with you and I would never make that mistake. You have to learn to love yourself before you can ever love anyone else. You have been hurt in your life and only you can fix that. But I am not a therapist and I'm not about to pretend to act like I know you."

He laughed, "stop acting like this. You were a scared little kitten when I first got you and now you want to act feisty. We both know that's not who you are."

"You don't know who I am. I will not be afraid to speak my mind because of who you are. Yes, you can kill me in a second. But I don't care about any of that because I know that I am right about everything that I'm saying. You keep hurting people because you were hurt and you never healed from it."

He stared at me for a second before finally releasing me. "Leave, you can take your brother and go because I have business to take care of. I'm giving you two hours to get the hell out."

I was shocked that he was letting me go because I didn't think that he would. But I knew that I couldn't sit here wasting time, I had to gather the little things that I had and get my brother so we could go. I was happy to finally get away from the man that turned my world upside down. But I was happy because I didn't get close to him. I couldn't help but feel bad for Athena because I knew deep in my heart that she went through a lot trying to love him. I wasn't sure of their history or the type of relationship that they had, but I just had a feeling. I got down from the pool table and headed out the room so that I could go prepare my things.

VAIN

I paced back-and-forth trying my best to get my thoughts under control. Aya was right, I didn't care about the games anymore. The only thing on my mind was what my father told me the other day. I had to think about what I wanted to do. Did I want to go back into Athena's life and turn it upside down for my pleasure? Did I want to start a war with Satoni because of the past? I had to ask myself all these questions because there would be consequences for my actions. I had enough on my plate and I didn't need to add more. But the thought of Athena being happy with him caused me to be angry somewhere deep down inside. All this time I kept denying that it was love but could it be? Thinking back to all the times that I told her that I loved her, was it real? I ran my fingers through my hair and laid down in bed. I needed to rest because I felt like my brain was going to explode. I took a deep breath and closed my eyes allowing myself to drift off to sleep.

Vain...Vain...Vain...Vain...

I blinked a few times and opened my eyes slowly. I was laying down in the grass and the sun was shining brightly in the sky. I frowned and looked around to see Isabella sitting next to me. I sat up quickly and she smiled at me.

"You're finally awake. I was waiting for you to open your eyes."

"How did you get here? Is this real?"

She giggled, "I'm dead so there is no way that this can be real. But I miss you and I wanted to see your face."

Before I could stop myself I pulled her into my arms. "I'm glad that you're okay. I haven't been able to stop thinking about you."

"That's a lie," she whispered. "You met someone else and you love her."

I pulled away so that I could look at her. "No, you have my heart. You will always have my heart."

"I'm dead, Vain. You can't live like this forever. I'm glad that you loved me and that helped me die in peace. I hate that I'm not going to be able to give you the life that you wanted, but you can move on. I won't hold you back anymore."

"No, no...there is no one that will ever make me feel the way that you did."

She grabbed my hand and kissed it, "you did. You treated her badly and she left you, but you care about someone more than me."

"It's not Athena," I cut her off quickly.

"It is," she whispered. "You fell in love with her, Vain and you know it. Stop being in denial about it because it doesn't make it easier. You loved her, but you let her go because you knew that you couldn't protect her. You didn't want her sharing the same fate that I have. You wanted to make sure that she was in the right hands and you did the right thing. But walking around acting like you didn't love her, is not true. She is your ex-fiancé just like me. You got down on one knee and asked her to marry you. You cherished her and for once I felt so happy to see you moving on. You can't stay stuck on me and what we had. Don't get me wrong, it's hard seeing you move on knowing that I'm dead and you're still alive, but you need to heal. You need time to really heal from what happened between all of us. Satoni lost his sister."

"Because she didn't want me to move on."

She placed her hand on my cheek, "no. She loved you. She loved you so much that she couldn't live with seeing you with someone else."

"But she lied to me and cheated on me." I sighed looking away.

"I know, but you have to move on. You can't keep living in the past. You got your revenge and then it turned around to be karma because you fell in love. Don't let what happened to me destroy your life. I have finally come to terms with everything and although my death wasn't fair, I'm okay with it."

"Did it hurt?" I whispered?

She shook her head, "no. They killed me and then beheaded me. My death was quick and painless. Satoni wasn't the one who pulled the trigger. He didn't want to kill me but he knew that his father wanted me dead. He was upset that his sister was dead, but he didn't want to hurt anyone else. Emilio lost his wife because she lost her daughter. I know that it sounds crazy, but it all happened and it needed to happen so that you don't make the same mistake again. If you continue to go to war with Satoni, more women will die. Athena has a son now; you can't kill his mother. I know what your father is asking of you, but you shouldn't do it."

I respected what she was saying but I couldn't help but wonder if my father played a part. Would she know? If she knew, would she be honest?

"Did my father play a part in her death?"

She stared down at her hands before replying, "yes. He made sure that she knew that you and I were engaged. He pushed her further and further into depression. I should have told you, but I didn't think you cared. Any time that I tried to bring her up, you would get upset. But now I know that I should have said something."

I pulled her into another hug and kissed the top of her head. "Thank you, I needed this more than you know."

She smiled, "I'm glad that I was able to help. Remember, healing starts with you and you have to want to. I held on to your heart long enough and it's time that I gave it back.

I opened my eyes quickly and looked around the dark room. I placed my hand on my chest, and for the first time in a long time it was pounding so hard I could hear it. Was that a dream or was it real?

I hope you all enjoyed this chapter

TELL ME

- -

I sat in my chair and stared up at the ceiling. My glass was half filled with bourbon and I lost count of how many glasses I had drank. I was tired...mentally tired and it seemed like nothing was working out for me. My father kept calling me but I didn't have the energy to talk to him. Today was my last day with my therapist and I thought that I would be happy. She wasn't helping me and it was a waste of my time. There was no reason why I should sit here and pour my heart out to her when I didn't have one. I was just like my father, but even he had a small piece of humanity left in him. He loved my mother more than anything. When he lost her, he left things to me just so he could be with her. What made him change? Why did he care so much about my mother leaving? He always told me that it was better to abandon all feelings. He said that they made you weak but I didn't believe that. He was doing the complete opposite of what he told me. He cherished the ground that mother walked on and respected her opinion. But he told me not to trust women because all they do is lie. I closed my eyes and sighed, what was I supposed to do? I smiled and thought back to Athena getting married. That was a special moment in her life and seeing me there shocked her. It made her angry, but I didn't care.

I mouthed the words forever and always and she stared at me with so much hate. I couldn't help but smirk and walk away. Their wedding was beautiful and I expected no less. I glanced over my shoulder to see her kissing Satoni and I balled my hands into fists. Why was I so angry? This is what I wanted, right? Why was I even here? All of this was so stupid. She moved on and I was supposed to be happy about it. She was no longer my problem and I played the part that I was supposed to. But there was something that kept me connected to her. I wanted to leave her, but I couldn't. It was the most annoying feeling in the world.

The wedding turned into a big celebration that continued until the moon came out. I was standing in the gazebo with my hands in my pockets. I could hear everyone dancing, laughing, and cheering. I kept my distance because I didn't want anyone to know that I was here. I smiled when I heard footsteps behind me. I knew that she would come to me.

"I'm sad that you didn't invite me to your wedding."

"Why would I invite you," she growled. "Why are you here? You should be lucky that I don't have you taken off the property. Have you lost your mind, Vain?"

I turned around to face her. She was standing there looking as beautiful as always. Her long hair was blowing lightly in the wind. She was wearing a white dress with no straps that sparkled in the night. She was breathtaking and I couldn't take my eyes off her. She walked up to me quickly and I could feel her anger. She was angry with me and she had every right to be.

"Why are you here?" She said through clenched teeth.

"I wanted to see you. I miss you, Amore. You look beautiful." I loved the look of shock upon her face as her eyes widened and met mine.

She stepped back as if I had just threatened her. "Don't call me that. I am not your love, and I want you to leave."

I chuckled, "you hurt me, Athena."

"I don't know what sick game you are playing, but you are insane. I would never give my heart to you again. You are an asshole. You are crazy, and I don't want you near my family."

As I stared at her I couldn't find the right words to say to her. I wanted to respond and say that I was sorry, but I wasn't. She tried to walk away, but I stopped her. She tried to get away from me, but I wasn't going to let her. I pinned her against the wooden wall of the gazebo and she gasped lightly.

"You didn't think I would leave without kissing the bride, did you?" I whispered in her ear.

"If you even think about putting your lips on mine, I will."

"Shhh," I whispered sucking her earlobe into my mouth. "You never fail to amaze me with your temper. You want to know something," I smiled pulling away to look into her eyes. "It's not that you don't want me here. The real problem is you want me. You want me too much and you are ready to nearly beg me to fuck you, despite your wish to remain faithful to your new husband."

"I don't want you, Vain. What part don't you understand? I will never be yours, so move on, and leave me alone."

"I told you before that you belonged to me, no matter what. Did you think that had changed? Do you think that I care about your marriage to him?" I smiled placing a kiss on her bare shoulder.

Her hands pushed against my shoulders in an attempt to push me away. "Vain, stop it." The tears that filled her eyes had spilled over and were now sliding down her cheeks. I stepped away from her and closed my eyes. "You have no idea what you have put me through. You hurt me, lied to me, abused me, and you keep tormenting me. Why? What do you want from me, Vain? Why do you keep doing this? You don't love me and you know it. So, why do you keep trying to make my life a living hell? Are you even sorry about everything that you did to me?"

"No," I said simply. "I'm not sorry about a damn thing. This is who I am, and that will never change."

She stared at me in disbelief. "I feel sorry for you then." She fixed her dress quickly and wiped away her tears. "Don't come back, ever. I will tell my husband if you continue to stalk me. I don't love you, Vain. You can go to hell because that's where you belong."

I watched her walk away and I didn't even think about stopping her. She would come back to me, she always did. I smiled and turned back to face the moon.

I opened my eyes when I heard my room door open. I looked over to see Aya walking in. I was confused because she was supposed to be gone. I left the check on the table and she was free to leave. I had a driver waiting for her whenever she was ready to leave.

"Why are you here?"

It seemed like she was debating with herself on how to answer that question. But she smiled and took another step towards me. "I was coming by to make sure that you were okay."

I frowned, "I'm fine. Get out."

"Listen, it's easy to be heartless because of who you are, but you can care about people."

I smirked and lifted my glass to my lips downing the alcohol inside. "Why? Caring has done nothing for me. I don't care about anything, Aya. You should know that by now."

"If you keep this up, you will lose everyone around you, and you will never find a woman to love you."

I sighed and sat up slowly, "who cares about love. Leave now before I change my mind."

She stared down at her feet before holding her head up high. I knew that she wasn't going to leave without a fight. "Isabella wouldn't want to see you like this."

I frowned and stood up slowly, "how do you know about her?"

"Well...I...I saw an old photo album and when I looked inside I saw photos of the two of you. You loved her and you lost her because of Satoni."

"That's none of your business and you shouldn't go through my things. Just because you see things, it doesn't mean they are real."

She shook her head, "you're drunk." She walked over to my bed and started to pull the covers back. I watched her in silence as she fluffed the pillows. She looked at me and pointed towards the bed. "You need to rest."

I rolled my eyes, "you don't tell me what to do. I think it's cute that you want to help, but you can't help me. You are my prisoner remember?"

She placed her hand on her hip, "get in the bed right now. You are being stubborn and that's one of your biggest issues."

I wanted to continue to argue with her but she was right. The alcohol was starting to kick in and I needed to lay down. I walked over to my bed and climbed in. I stared at the ceiling as she pulled the blanket over me. She reminded me so much of Athena when she acted like this.

"Have you ever been in love before?" I asked closing my eyes.

"No, I've been too focused on college. But I know how it feels to lose someone that you love. When my parents died, I was lost. I stopped living because I felt like why should I? But my best friend taught me that life goes on and the people we love wouldn't want to see us this way. They would want us to live life and move on."

"Parents and a girlfriend are two different things. Isabella died so gruesomely and it had nothing to do with her. There are so many questions that I don't have the answer to. If I could go back in time...would I change anything? I'm not sure."

She shook her head, "get some rest. I'm sure that all the answers that you need will come to you at the right time."

I grabbed her hand before she could walk away. "Aya, will you sit with me for a few more minutes." My request shocked her, but she didn't hesitate to take a seat beside me. I inhaled deeply and pulled her close. "You smell really good," I mumbled.

"You're saying that because you're drunk," she whispered.

"I just wanted to protect her. I thought that I had all the power in the world but I couldn't protect her. She died because of me and the only thing I want to do is forget that she ever existed. Every time I think of her...it hurts. I hate feeling weak, lost, and incomplete, but that's the way I feel. I've felt this way ever since I lost her. No one can fill the void in me." I don't know where all off this was coming from. But maybe it was because of the alcohol. They always said that a drunk man tells the truth. I opened my eyes and frowned, "I destroy any woman who gets close to me. Because loving me means their death."

She grabbed my hand and squeezed it, "that's not true. You have to heal, Vain."

I smirked, "heal?" I had heard that word a lot lately. But how would I even start? Where would I go for healing? A therapist couldn't help me, and I felt like I was at the end of my road. "Tell me how?"

"You have to go back and confront your sadness and loneliness. It didn't start with Isabella. It started in your childhood. You have to start living for yourself and not for everyone else. I hope that maybe one day you are able to find what you are looking for."

My eyes felt heavy and I couldn't think straight any more. I knew that Aya was sitting right next to me but she sounded so far away.

"Athena," I whispered, before finally allowing darkness to consume me.

I hope you all enjoyed this chapter

CHIARA

I stared around the dark room confused. Where was I and why was I here? I looked around until I saw a girl with long black hair walking towards me. She was wearing a long white dress and I smiled. It was Athena, why was she here? The smile on my face quickly faded as she got closer and I realized that she was not Athena. She stopped in front of me and smiled and I couldn't stop myself. I grabbed her by the throat and she laughed. Why was she here and what the hell did she want?

"Vain, you're hurting me." She pouted sticking her bottom lip out.

"What the hell do you want, Chiara."

She cocked her head to the side and smiled, "I've really missed you, Vain."

Before I could respond, I heard Athena's voice. I turned around to see that we were in my club. Athena was standing there in a blue dress with matching heels. I released Chiara and waited to see what would happen.

"I-I'm sorry...I didn't mean...I thought that you were someone else." She turned to leave but I stopped her.

"What is your name?"

"I'm Athena," she whispered. I told the girl I was kissing to leave. She walked past her and bumped her shoulder aggressively.

Chiara walked over to Athena and rubbed her cheek gently. "She is beautiful. You always had really good taste in women."

Before I could respond the room changed and now I was standing in the dance studio that now belonged to Athena.

"Vain I said no," she struggled against me.

"I just want to feel you, just for a minute. Let me put it in at least once. I promise I won't hurt you." I stood there and watched as I slammed her down on the desk and yanked her legs open.

Chiara walked towards the desk shaking her head. "No means no, Vain. You should know that by now."

I balled my hands into fists and turned to face her. "I didn't rape her."

"But you would have, I mean that is the devil that you are, right?"

Before I could respond we were in another place. I quickly recognized this place as the beach condo I took Athena to.

"Wait...don't you need a condom?"

I looked into her eyes and sighed. "No, I want to feel you. It's your first time and I want us to enjoy it." Before she could protest, I kissed her roughly and she whimpered feeling me start to enter her. I broke the kiss and groaned burying my face in her neck.

"Vain...ouch," she closed her eyes tight.

"Relax," that's all I said before sucking her nipple into my mouth.

"You finally got what you wanted. But you knew exactly what you were doing, Vain. You made her feel like she could trust you. You had her at her most vulnerable moment and you preyed on that. But that's what you do best."

"Why are you showing me all of this? What are you trying to gain?"

She laughed, "you want answers and I am going to give them to you. I want to show you who you really are."

The room changed and now I was in Athena's room.

"You have a lovely home." I smirked, "you have nothing to say?"

"Vain, get out. You have no right to come into my home. You have no right to stalk me, I'm not your property." She turned around and tried to run but before she could reach the bathroom, I yanked her by the hair roughly.

"You are such an ungrateful bitch. I took you to Spain and spoiled you the whole time there. I bought that Condo for sixty thousand dollars for you. I let you spend one thousand dollars on clothes for yourself. I told you that I loved you. You get angry about some text messages on my phone and ignore me. You ignore me after everything that I've done for you, really?"

"She had every right to try to escape you, Vain. But you won't ever put your pride to the side. Your true colors started to show and she saw that. Instead of leaving her alone, what do you do? Well, let's see." She snapped her fingers and the room changed.

"Stop lying to me, Amore. I know that you opened your legs to him. You opened your legs so easily to me." I licked my lips and grabbed her towel yanking it away from her body.

She balled her hands into fists and covered herself. "Get out. Get out of my house now. I will call my brother and tell him that."

"Tell him how I fucked you. Tell him how I almost got you pregnant," I chuckled. I grabbed her and pulled her against my body. "Tell him how many times I've been inside you while you're at it." I stroked her cheek with the back of my hand softly. "You will learn not to threaten me."

"You said that she was a slut for going out on a date. Why did you feel that way? You were having sex with Lina at the time. Am I wrong, Vain?"

I couldn't deny it because it was true. I had no reason to act like that towards Athena, but I did. She snapped her fingers again and this time, Athena was sitting at a table with Satoni.

"Baby girl, thank you for your company. Here is a little something to show my gratitude." He pulled something out his jacket pocket and slowly stuck it in the middle of her boobs. He cupped her chin forcing her to look at him. "stai attento...ti fidi facilmente."

"You didn't even realize that your enemy was in your club to finally claim his bride. But it didn't matter to you anyway because you got what you wanted, right? But if you did, why did you do this?" She snapped her fingers again and the room changed.

"VAIN PLEASE I'M NOT LYING...YOU'RE HURTING ME!"

I threw her on the ground roughly, "I want a name and I want it now."

She shook her head and crawled into the corner, "I don't know...please I don't know."

"You hated the thought of her being with another man. You didn't even care that she was taken by Satoni. Well, that was until he proposed to her. You are selfish, Vain. You only care about yourself and you know it. Even when I think of Isabella, it's the same thing. You act like you loved her so much, but you hurt her too. Should I refresh your memory?" She snapped her fingers.

"Vain, you're hurting me."

I had Isabella pinned to the bed and she was struggling against me. "Why are you dressed like a whore? I told you not to wear that dress and you did it anyway."

"You can't tell me how to dress."

I pinned her hands above her head, "you are mine."

She snapped her fingers again.

"I am your fiancé."

I smirked before grabbing her by the throat. "My fiancé? You are much more than that. You will be my wife and I expect you to play your part. You represent me. You will never embarrass me like that in front of my father."

Tears slid down her cheeks as she nodded quickly. I released her and left the room quickly. She sank to her knees crying.

"It has always been about your father. You wanted to make him proud and you didn't care who you hurt in the process." She snapped her fingers again.

"Is this what you want," she whispered wrapping the sheet around her body. "You want to see me like this? You want to hurt me...rape me...for what? To please your father?"

I stared up at the ceiling debating with myself on what I should say to her. There was nothing that I could say. I was turning into a monster, and I didn't know why.

Again, the snap of her fingers changed our surroundings.

"What the hell is this?" Isabella asked looking down at the cocaine on the table.

"I told you not to come in here," I growled.

"Yeah, I see why. You're doing drugs, Vain. Have you lost your mind?"

"It's none of your business, get out now."

"It is my business, you're my soon to be husband. I don't want a drug addict for a spouse." She turned to walk away but I stopped her.

"You would blame it on the drugs because you knew it was easier. But they didn't make you into the devil that you are. You were born to be one just like your father."

Once again I found myself in a familiar place. Women were walking around serving drinks to men at the club. I was fifteen and my father wanted me here. He said that this was going to be mine one day and I needed to know how to run it. He was sitting with Emilio, Sergio, and Alonzo. They were laughing and having drinks. It was weird watching him play nice with them when he knew that he wanted to kill them. He looked at me and winked and I smiled at him. He was someone that I inspired to be. He was a man to be feared and respected and I wanted to be just like him.

"I can see the light in your eyes, you were so young and naïve. You loved your father, but he treated you like nothing but a soldier." She snapped her fingers again. "Oh, now we get to go down memory lane with me. But our relationship was short lived. We both know that you treated me badly."

"You deserved it, and you know it. I didn't want to be with you, Chiara. You can call it what you want, but you tried to pin a baby on me that wasn't mine. You took your own life because you wanted to hurt Isabella."

She giggled, "do you think that's what happened?"

I frowned, "that's exactly what happened. I let you go and you didn't want to accept it. It's not my fault that you couldn't find love, Chiara. You know that our relationship was forced to better the relationship between Emilio and my father. You didn't love me; you loved the power that came with me."

She rolled her eyes, "you know...you're so full of yourself. It was never about love, Vain. It was about power, but not for me. I wanted to spare you the truth, but it's the truth you seek...so I will give it to you." She snapped her fingers and I frowned. We were in my father's bedroom.

"Please, I'm begging you." She whispered.

"Will Emilio seal the deal or not?"

"He said no, I don't know what else you want me to do. I tried to get him to change his mind. But he wants to give half of Italy to the Vintalli family. I told him that it would be better to give it to me, but he said no. Satoni will marry Athena, it has already been signed off on."

He walked up to her and grabbed her by the throat. "What do I have to do to make him give me what I want."

"I...I don't know. My step father is a very stubborn man. He doesn't want me to be with Vain and I'm doing everything I can to convince him that I want to marry into your family."

I frowned, "what the hell was that about?"

She smiled weakly, "your father wanted me to be with you. He wanted me to marry you so that he could have fifty percent of Italy. But my step father wasn't dumb and he saw right through Victor." She snapped her fingers again.

I was sitting across the dinner table from Athena. I was showing her all of the evidence that I had against Satoni.

"What about you? You killed Satoni's sister and never looked back."

I sat up straight slowly, "listen to me. I don't know what he told you but I never killed his sister. The truth is, we were together and I loved her but she had problems. Problems that I couldn't fix no matter how hard I tried. I may be an asshole but I wasn't always this way. The relationship was great at first, but then she changed. She started being very possessive of me. If I did something that she didn't like she would threaten to kill herself. She told me that I had to marry her or she would kill herself. She was a suicidal mess and I couldn't deal with it anymore. She wanted me to get her pregnant and I said no. We were just kids and I wasn't ready for a baby. My father was on my back about running the family and then there was her. She started to cheat on me with a guy named James Franco. She got pregnant by him and tried to tell me that it was my baby. As hard as it was for me, I ended the relationship. My family and I couldn't take any more of her. Two months after we broke up, I fell in love again. I thought that we were moving on and things were getting better but then my girlfriend started receiving letters from her." I pulled a few letters out of the folder and handed them to her.

"Now, let's break down this story that you told her." She sighed sitting down on the table.

I hope that you all enjoyed this chapter

BLACKMAIL

"So, I feel like it will be better to start from the beginning. I didn't love you. The only reason that we started to date was because your father blackmailed me. Blue took advantage of me and I became pregnant. I didn't want anything to do with him, and so I got an abortion. Yes, I'm talking about the same Blue that attacked Athena. Victor found out and threatened to tell my stepfather. He told me that I was going to help him and I felt like at that time I didn't have any other choice. So, I came onto you and before I knew it we were in a relationship. Throughout the whole relationship, he was constantly blackmailing me. He wanted me to get you to love me so that you would propose to me and then once we were married, he could have half of Italy. He wanted me to keep trying to convince Emilio. But he was a smart man and he always had a plan. His plan was for Satoni and Athena to marry. He had already sealed the deal with Alonzo so there was nothing that I could do. I thought that once your father figured out that there was no hope, he would let me go. But he didn't and I don't know why I thought that he would. At this point you didn't desire me anymore and we were fighting all the time. We were fighting because I was miserable, and I didn't want to do any of this. You started dating Isabella and I finally saw hope at the end of the road. I thought that now that you had found someone that really made you happy, he would leave me alone. But once again Victor would stop at nothing to get what he wanted. He made me say those things and write those things. He wanted me to do anything to get you back and that included playing like I was suicidal. The truth is, I did move on with James Franco. I got pregnant and I was happy because I finally felt free. But it was short-lived because your father came back again blackmailing me. He told me that he wanted me to pin the child on you. I didn't want to do it but I knew that my life would never be the same if my father found out about my abortion. So, I did what I had to do. Every time that I did it, I felt sick to my stomach. I never wanted to ruin a happy home. It got to the point where I finally gathered up the courage to confront Victor. I told him that I didn't want to do any of this anymore, and I didn't care if he told my step-father about what was going on. I felt like it was the best decision that I ever made, but I was wrong. When I decided to stop working for him, he treated me like a threat. I had too much information on him and you know your father better than I do. He will do whatever it takes to tie up the loose end and that's exactly what I was to him at that point. I knew that he was going to destroy me and I was scared. I knew what I had done, and I didn't want to face my father or you after everything that happened. So, I decided to take my own life. It was the one thing that I felt like I could control at that point. Victor had taken all that he could take from me, and I didn't desire to be here anymore. But before I died, I had one last phone call with Victor. He didn't hesitate to tell me what his new plan was now that I was out of the picture. He told me that my death would cause a war. When he said that I started to second-guess myself and tell myself not to do it. But at the same time, I felt like if I didn't, I would continue to be controlled by him."

I took a step back watching as sadness washed over her face. I had no idea that she was going through all of this, and it was because of my father. To know that he had taken advantage of her sickened me.

"I wanted to tell you what was going on, but I was afraid. He told me that you wouldn't believe me and that you were his son. You would always take his word over mine, and I knew it was true. He knew exactly what he was doing. But what I hate the most is the fact that he used my death, my freedom to continue to hurt you. He took something from me that was not his to take. I thought that if I died, that would be the end of it. But all he did was forge a letter to make my family believe that you did me so wrong that I killed myself. Your father knew that Emilio and Satoni would want revenge. He knew that they would kill Isabella. He knew that he could then use Athena to even the score. Your father doesn't just think about the moment. He plans years and years ahead and that's what makes him so scary. He preyed on Isabella and Athena. He wanted to keep hurting Satoni and the Vintalli family as much as he could. And he used you to do it. It was his idea for you to take Athena's virginity."

As I sat there and listened to what she said, it all made sense. My father was a very calculated man. Every move that he made, it had to make sense. He didn't want me to be with Isabella, and so he did what he had to do to get her out of the picture. He wanted me to be with Chiara, but I declined.

He doesn't care about anyone but himself. If you would have married Athena, trust me when I tell you this. He would have found a way to kill her. You love her and you know that you do. He is threatened by Athena's very existence. Because she is the one that's in the way of what he wants. When he found out that Satoni and Athena were to be married, he turned into a monster. He said... that little bitch is taking away everything that I worked hard for. He said that he wanted to see her head in a box like Isabella. You wanted the truth and now you have it. It is completely up to you what you do with it. But your father is not your hero, he is much worse."

"I don't know what to believe," I whispered. I hated that I was getting all of this information all at once. None of it made sense anymore. My father was power hungry, but would he go this far?

"He is the one that hired Blue to attack Athena that night. I know that you won't believe me because I'm dead, but I'm telling you the truth."

"Why?' I growled.

"It was a test. He wanted to see if you loved Athena, and you proved to him that you did. All of this was a set up by him. He was even using Tarma against you and Satoni. He was blackmailing her until the very end. She died because of him, not during child birth. I know that it's a lot to take in, but you have to believe me. He wants Athena gone and he will use you to do it. When he can't use you, he will use other people. You and Satoni fought back and forth about the Alba Rosa because you didn't really know the truth. Satoni played his part, you played yours, but you both were a piece on Victor's board game."

I balled my hands into fists and closed my eyes. I was growing more and more pissed off by the second. "What are his plans now? Do you know?"

"I know that he wants you to kill Athena. I'm telling you not to do it. If you kill Athena, Satoni will destroy New York. He will stop at nothing to get revenge. Everything that the mafia has worked hard for, will be destroyed. The four mafia families will become a target for the Russian mafia. You have to remain strong and united. You have to let the past be in the past and stop living under your father's commands."

I ran my fingers through my hair slowly. "Chiara, would you lie to me?"

"I have nothing to gain. I'm here because you want the truth and I wanted to give it to you. I want to rest in peace and I can't seem to do that. I am a part of you whether you want to admit it or not. If you don't start healing, you'll hurt Athena. I know that you don't want to do that. You love her more than anything, Vain. You love her so much, and you deserve to have that feeling."

"But she is not mine. I will never be with her."

"I know, but you got to experience something with her. She is the key to holding the mafia together. She was born for a reason and it's time that you start to appreciate her. Your father is trying to destroy something so beautiful because he is stuck in his ways. But this is not about him anymore."

She had a point. My father was stuck in the old ages, and that wouldn't benefit us. But I couldn't stop thinking about the deal that he was trying to make with the Russian Mafia. "He wants to make a deal with them."

She frowned, "what do you mean?"

"He wants me to go meet with the Russian Mafia to negotiate a deal."

Her eyes widened, "no. Don't do it. They only want to over throw all of you and he knows that. Whatever he is trying to do can't be good. You need to stop him, Vain. He has destroyed the lives of so many people. Kylie Rivers, that was him too. He had his men kidnap her and then place her in the pick-up area for Emilio's men. He will stop at nothing to try to frame, destroy, and humiliate the Romano and Vintalli family."

I woke up to my phone buzzing and I looked around my room. Aya was gone, and my head was pounding. Was that a dream or was that real? I looked down to see that it was my father. I answered the phone quickly because I had a lot of questions for him.

"I've been trying to reach you all damn day. What the hell have you been doing. That's not the point, have you made a decision about Athena yet?"

"Before I tell you what my answer is, I have some questions for you. Why did you blackmail Chiara? And why is Isabella dead because of you?"

The phone went silent and I raised an eyebrow. "How do you know about that?"

My heart felt like it stopped beating. So, he wasn't going to deny that he was behind all of this? What the hell was my father doing, and why was he doing things like this behind my back. My blood was boiling and I knew that I was going to do something crazy. I would kill him if he didn't start talking soon. I wanted answers and he was going to give them to me. Then I would let him know that I wasn't going to kill Athena. I'm sure that would piss him off, but I didn't care. I was going to trust Chiara because I had a feeling that she wasn't lying to me. Everything that she said made a lot of sense to me.

I hope you all enjoyed this chapter

I LOVE YOU

I caught a flight to Spain early in the morning because I wanted to see my father face to face. I wanted him to look me in my eyes and confess his sins and lies to me. I waited for him to speak and the silence was killing me. I was done with the lies and all the bullshit that came with him. I wanted to know the truth and I wanted to know right now. He sighed and gulped down the alcohol in his glass. I could tell by the way that he was acting that he was shocked that I found out. But none of that mattered to me now.

"If you want the truth, I'll give it to you. Yes, I was the one who blackmailed Chiara. I didn't want you to be with Isabella."

I felt like my heart stopped in my chest. "Did you know that Isabella would die?"

"Yes, I knew because Emilio had wrote me a letter after his wife died. I knew that they were coming for her and so I tipped him off when she went shopping with Alondra. It was perfect because you didn't send security with them."

I ran my fingers through my hair, "you did all of this because you wanted to use Athena. You wanted to have a reason to use me to continue to have a grudge against them."

"Yeah, I won't lie about it. I knew that it would play out well in the end. But I wasn't expecting you to fall in love with Athena. That's what ruined the plan. If you would just do what I say, you would see that I know what I'm doing."

I had enough of his bullshit. "No, all of this is because of you. You don't understand what you did because you can't stand to be in the spot you're in. You killed five innocent women because you wanted to hurt the Vintalli family and the Romano family. We can't control the past and where we were placed in the ranks. If you really wanted to move up, you should have done it the right way."

He chuckled, "what's the right way? Son, you know as well as I do that they weren't going to side with us."

"They won't work with us because of you. You push everyone away because you look at them as if they are beneath us. I don't want any parts of what you have going on anymore. You are going to destroy everything that we worked hard for trying to get the Russian mafia to do business with you. What is the deal that you made with them anyway?"

He shrugged, "that's none of your business."

I growled and stood up, "does it involve Athena?"

"Why does it matter to you?"

I didn't understand my father. Why was Athena on his hit list? Why did he want to hurt her so badly? "Why are you doing this? Why are you scared of a woman?"

"You don't know your history do you? You see, Alonzo and I have a long history of broken promises. When his wife was carrying Roman, his wife went into labor with him early. He didn't think that she was going to make it and so he said that if he didn't have a successor, everything would go to me. We were friends and he trusted me with his life."

That couldn't be right, he hated them. "That's impossible. You hated the Vintalli family and you know it. How could you possibly be their friend?"

He held his hand up, "I met him before he married Gia. Anyway, Roman was born and every one celebrated. I wasn't really thrilled about it, but what could I do. Gia was told that she would not be able to have kids anymore. But she magically got pregnant and it was a girl this time. The mafia was going crazy for two reasons. Number one, if Roman died, she would take his place. They didn't think that a woman would be fit for the mafia. Number two, she was the first girl born to a mafia leader in twenty years. Sergio wanted Athena to become a part of his family. But he only wanted her to provide an heir for Adonis. Emilio wanted Satoni to marry Athena so that he could strengthen the Vintalli family. You were supposed to marry Chiara, but you met Isabella. Once I saw that plan was gone, I used Satoni's soon-to-be bride to even the score. I want what was promised to me before that little bitch was born."

I rubbed my forehead, "so you killed Chiara, Isabella, Alondra, Tarma and Kylie?"

"I did what I had to do."

"And it still failed," I turned to leave the room. I had enough of his bullshit. I was going to fix all of this because I was done with the fighting.

"I always get what I want, Vain. You should know that about me."

I looked over my shoulder at him, "stop. You are causing more damage within the family. You are making us look bad because you are power hungry."

"You are my son and you should see my side of it. Who cares if we kill a few little whores along the way. It is all for a greater cause."

"More money? That's the greater cause? That's where you are mistaken, money won't get me back the woman that I loved." I walked out of his office and slammed the door. I was done with my father; it was time to over throw him completely.

It has been a week since I talked to my father and now he was inviting me to dinner. I decided to stay in Spain for a little while longer. It was annoying, but I needed to gather as much information as I could. I walked into the backyard but I stopped in my tracks when I saw Athena standing there. She was wearing a long white dress and she was pregnant. Her large baby bump couldn't be hidden and I couldn't stop myself from feeling a little jealous. So, she was pregnant again? I shook my head and looked her up and down slowly. Her hands were tied in front of her and her eyes widened when she saw me. I frowned and took a step towards her, but she stepped back. I looked behind her and noticed that she was standing in front of the pool. If she took a few more steps back, she would fall in.

"Why are you doing this?" I could see that her cheeks were stained from crying. She looked at me with so much hate and I didn't understand why. "Vain, you are the biggest mistake of my life. I wish that I would have never met you. You won't let me go even when I beg you to, and it's because you are so obsessed with me. I don't want to be with you, Vain. Why can't you accept that, huh? Why are you doing this to me? I have lost everything because of you. I lost my best friend, I lost my senior year in high school, I lost my home, I lost my life and you still want to torture me. I hate you so much, and I want you to get that through your head."

It pissed me off hearing her say the things that she was saying, but that wasn't why I was here. I was coming to meet my father, why the hell was she here? "Why are you here?"

"Don't play stupid, Vain. You kidnapped me."

I took a step towards her, but she stepped back. I held my hands up in surrender trying to get her to stay still. "Athena, listen to me. I didn't kidnap you. This was not something that I would have done."

"And you expect me to believe you?"

"You need to," I cut her off. I knew that I needed her to listen to me. The only way that I was going to do that was to be honest with her. "Athena, look...I'm sorry about everything that I did to you. I know that I have hurt you, lied to you, abused you, and so much more. But I would never hurt you...not again. I need you to trust me because right now your life depends on it." I walked up to her and for once she didn't step away. "I love you," I whispered grabbing her hand. "I love you so fucking much that I...I tried not to. You drive me crazy and I was searching for an escape because I didn't want to lose you. If I'm not honest than history will repeat itself." She looked away, but I cupped her chin forcing her to look at me. "I wanted to protect you, and that's why I pushed you away. I knew that if you loved me, you would die. As much as I wanted to be with you, I couldn't. You were not mine to take, and I knew that you would be safer with Satoni. I know that all of this is confusing, but I found out the truth. We were all a part of my father's sick game and he preyed on the fact that I loved you. He was the one who killed Tarma."

She gasped and shook her head, "What?"

"I know that it's a lot, but I'll explain it later."

"Why am I here?" she whispered.

"I don't know, but I'm going to get you back home." I grabbed her hands and tried to untie the ropes, but I noticed that they were tied and locked with a padlock. I needed the code to open it. I cursed under my breath and sighed.

"I'm glad that you made it, son. Do you like your gift?" My father smirked walking out of the house with a few men following behind him.

"What the hell are you doing? Why are you doing this to her?"

"I told you last week, I don't think that you were listening." I heard a girl scream and I looked over to see Azira being pushed down to the ground and a gun was placed on the back of her head.

"What the hell is she doing here?"

My father chuckled, "choose who you will protect. Who do you care about more, Athena, or your little booty call who looks like her?"

"You're making a mistake."

He shrugged and nodded at his men giving them the signal to proceed. The sound of the gun went off and Athena screamed. I closed my eyes quickly and gulped. This was not what was supposed to happen. I looked up to see Azira lying there in a pool of growing blood. I cursed under my breath and turned to face Athena. She tried to step away from me, but I grabbed her so she wouldn't fall. "Look at me, don't look away from me." It wasn't working because her eyes kept drifting from me to my father, and then to Azira.

"YOU'RE A MONSTER," She screamed. "YOU ARE FUCKING SICK AND TWISTED."

My father chuckled, "I will do whatever it takes to make sure my family survives."

"No, you will do whatever it takes to destroy Vain's life. You killed her because she was close to Vain, and you feel threatened by any woman who he gets close to."

I didn't want Athena arguing with him. It wasn't her place and she was only going to piss him off further.

My father stepped towards us and I pulled her close. "Athena, I did a lot of things I'm not proud of."

"Yeah, like killing my best friend. You're fucking scum."

She was just as feisty as the day that I met her. The mafia flowed through her veins and so did the Italian temper.

"I killed your parents too."

I looked up and I could feel Athena tense up. I had no idea that he was a part of their deaths. "Why?" She whispered.

"Once they were out of the picture, it made it easier for Vain to fuck you. You were so alone and vulnerable and it was all a part of my plan. Everything worked in my favor, and it still is."

"So, what's your plan now?"

He smirked, "kill you and take what was owed to me before your mother ruined it."

Everything happened so fast. He reached into his waistband and pulled out his gun. Before I could react, he fired, and Athena went falling to the ground.

I hope you all enjoyed this chapter

SEE YOU IN HELL

I caught her before she could hit the ground. Her white dress was slowly starting to turn red and I was panicking. She was looking at me and I cursed loudly placing my hand on her cheek.

"Vain," she whispered. "I...I'm sorry."

"Don't talk, just save your breath." I lifted her into my arms and was about to walk into the house but I was stopped by Adonis, Satoni, and Roman. They were all pointing their guns at me and I was frozen in place. I stared at them confused, but as I looked around I seen that my father was gone.

"Why?" Satoni growled. I could see the anger in his eyes as he gripped the gun tightly. His hand was on the trigger and he was ready to kill me.

"I didn't do it."

"Please, we all know how you work, Vain. You will stop at nothing to punish me and my sister. She wanted to move on, but you won't let her."

I knew that everyone was tired of me and all of my tricks, but I was telling the truth this time. "I didn't do it," I growled holding Athena close. "I know that you don't believe me, but I wouldn't hurt Athena. I have hurt her more than enough, but shooting a pregnant woman is low. I would never do something like that. You have to believe me."

"What the hell happened?" Adonis asked lowering his gun a little.

"It was all a part of my father's plan. He has been playing with all of us for years. He killed Tarma, Chiara, Kylie, Alondra, listen I know it sounds crazy. I can't explain it right now. We need to get her to the hospital. She is losing a lot of blood, and we can't waste another second."

They hesitated but lowered their guns and allowed me to run towards my car. I was scared, it was crazy feeling this way. It had been a long time since I was scared, and I hated the feeling. I wanted Athena to live and I wasn't sure if she would. I placed her in the backseat of the car and Satoni climbed in. Adonis climbed in next to him and Roman walked up to me. My hands were covered in her blood and I was shaking. Roman placed his hand on my shoulder and I looked into his eyes. I expected to see anger, but I saw that he was worried.

"Vain, I'll drive." I nodded my head and climbed into the passenger seat. He jumped in the driver's seat and backed out of the driveway quickly. My mind was running a mile a minute and my heart felt like it was going to explode. I didn't want another woman dying because of me.

We arrived at the hospital and they took Athena to the back. Satoni told them that she had been shot and that she was seven months pregnant. They told him that they would do everything that they could. All I could do was sit in a chair and stare across the room at the wall. My father got away and there was no telling where he was now. He shot Athena, and now he was gone. Fuck, why was all of this happening right now. I hated that Athena was dragged into all of this, and I hated that my father was behind it. There was no way that I was going to forgive him after this. He betrayed me and the family by hurting Athena. She didn't deserve any of this and he knew that. He was only thinking about himself, and it showed now more than ever.

"Vain, what happened."

I looked up to see Adonis sitting across from me. "I don't...I don't even." I gripped the chair for support before finally closing my eyes. When I opened my eyes I felt hot liquid running down my cheeks.

"Fuck," Adonis whispered, before grabbing me by the back of the neck and pulling me into a hug.

"I was going to have dinner with my father and she was there. He did all of this, he planned it all. He wanted you to think that I shot her." I pushed him away and stood up wiping my face. "I would never hurt her like that and you know it."

"I know, brother. Victor has been playing a dangerous game and now he is going to pay for it. We have our men out looking for him. When we catch him, what do you want us to do."

"Hold him until I get there. He is not going to get away with this. He killed their parents too. He has been playing with my emotions this whole time. I had no idea at all, Adonis. He was making sure that I kept you guys as an enemy. He didn't want me getting close to you unless it was good for him. I should have seen right through him, but I didn't."

Satoni walked into the waiting room and he looked a mess. I wanted to say something to him, but there was nothing that I could say. Before I could react he pulled me into a hug. I was shocked, but I hugged him back. We had never hugged before, and it was a strange feeling. We had been enemies since we were little.

"You were there for her and I appreciate it. I had no idea that your father was behind all of this."

"I'll tell you everything that I know."

We all sat down and I started to tell them about Chiara and Isabella. We had nothing but time as we waited to see what would happen to Athena.

Roman was drifting off to sleep and Satoni was on the phone with Giovanni. Adonis was talking to Asher about my father's whereabouts, and I was staring at the wall...waiting. We had been sitting here for four hours and I wanted to know what was going on with Athena. The doctor walked into the room and cleared his throat. We all stood up and his eyes widened.

"Well, Athena is in stable condition. The bullet grazed her side, but still did a little damage, but it missed any major veins and arteries. She was losing a lot of blood, so you got her here in good timing."

"Wait, what about the baby?" Satoni asked looking worried.

He smiled, "the baby is fine. It has a good heartbeat and seems to be stable as well. She is awake and she wanted to see you. If you follow me, I'll take you to her room."

We followed him out of the waiting room and down the hall. I was happy to hear that Athena was okay. I needed to see her now more than ever. I needed to explain to her that I had nothing to do with what happened. We walked into her room and she was propped up on her pillow with a tray of food in her lap. She smiled at us and we smiled back.

"I didn't know that my room would be filled with four mafia leaders."

We laughed a little and Satoni walked over to her and kissed her forehead. He placed his hand on her stomach, "I love you."

She smiled and kissed him, "I love you more. Oh, she tried to sit up quickly. "Vain, I'm sorry. I'm sorry that I said all of those things to you. I mean some of it was true, but I should have trusted you."

I smiled, "no. You had every right to be skeptical. I have done some fucked up shit to you. I just want you to know that I would never hurt you or try to kill you."

She smirked, "that means a lot. I feel like we need to heal from the past. All of us because we can't keep doing this. Our father's wanted us to be enemies, but we are all we have. I have a son now and he will take over things once Satoni steps down. I'm sure that one day you will have sons too, and I don't want my son to hate your kids. I want you to teach them how to love each other and work together, and that all starts with you. All of you need to leave the past in the past and get along. I hate what happened to the women that you loved, but we can't continue to have grudges because of it. We were all tricked by Victor and it's time that we fixed that. He has taken so much from us, and I fear what he will do next. I won't live in fear because of him. But I will protect my kids and my family against him. I know that he is your father, Vain, but he is a threat to me."

"I feel the same way," Satoni said sitting next to her. "I want to get along, but I won't have your father coming after my wife."

"Same," Roman said walking over to Satoni. "She is my sister and the only family that I have left."

"I feel the same way," Adonis sighed joining them. "I have had my fair share of causing hell. But Athena means a lot to Satoni and he is my brother. We might not be related by blood, but I will stand by his side."

I smiled, "then we all agree. My father was someone who I loved and looked up to. But he has taken so much from me and turned me into the man I am today. I will not continue to live the way that he wants me to. I will protect Athena and protect you guys too. This is the life that I want."

I knew what I had to do and I was going to do it because Athena wouldn't be hurt because of my father. I would not allow him to kill her because he wanted to create history. The war between the families was over, and we were going forward together. He wasn't going to ruin that anymore.

It has been a week since my father shot Athena and then went on the run. We have been actively searching for him and still didn't have a lead until finally Adonis called me. He said that they had found him in Colombia with my mother. I had him brought back to Spain, and now I was going to see him. I walked out onto the balcony and smiled at him. He was tied to a chair and he looked pissed off. I greeted him in Italian and he growled. The sun was shining and I could see the ocean directly behind us. That's what I loved most about this house. It was located right on the water, and being here brought me a lot of peace.

"I hope you know what you're doing?" He growled watching me take a seat in front of him.

"I do," I smiled. "I think that I have had a lot of time to think it through. You see, you destroyed my life. You took advantage of me time and time again. Used me to do your dirty work, and then through me under the bus to cover your own ass. You are not my father; you are my enemy. I told you not to hurt her, but you did anyway."

"You are going to risk it all for a whore, Vain?"

"She is the Queen of the Mafia. She has changed the way things are and I will forever be grateful to her. I love her, I love her so much. I loved Isabella and she was taken from me. I hurt Athena because of you, and now I'm stopping it. I will not lose another woman because of you."

He laughed, "women won't get you far."

"Say what ever you need to say to cover your own ass. But it won't change your fate. You can pray and repent for your sins, but you are still going to hell." I stood up slowly and placed my hands in my pockets. "I hated that you never treated me like a son. You never hugged me once; you saw me as your soldier. Now, I'm cutting all ties to you. You will never be mentioned in our history again because I'm going to remove everything about you. It will be as if you never existed. My future son will not know the devils that we became."

"Do what needs to be done, son. But I will see you in hell."

"No, that's where you will go." I grabbed my gun out of my waist and cocked it before placing it against his head. "Victor," I smiled, before pulling the trigger. His body went limp and blood covered him. He was dead and I was happy. I knew that my mother wouldn't understand, but I wasn't expecting her to.

I hope you all enjoyed this chapter

It was hard telling my mother about what I had done. I knew that she would be disappointed in me and hate me for killing the love of her life. But I needed her to understand that it was for the best. She didn't take the news well and she slapped me. But after crying out all the tears that she could, she told me that she understood.

I had to protect myself and the family name. I wouldn't let my father take that from us because that's all that we had left. She knew that it hurt me because I loved my father. I wanted him to be a real father to me instead of being my boss. I wanted him to look at me and value me as his son. I did everything that I could to make him proud, but never even got a good job son. He controlled every part of my life, even my future without me knowing. My father was my idol and I looked up to him. I would've never thought that he would be the one to cause me so much pain and suffering. He made me into the person that I am today but now that he was gone I feel like I could be myself. I wasn't putting all the blame on him though because there were times when I was just a fucked-up person because I wanted to be. I hurt Athena because I wanted to. I wanted to be with her so badly and I hated that I couldn't. I wanted to punish her for not being fully Italian.

The truth is...No, I don't see myself changing overnight and I know that it will take time, but I'm open to it. I learned a lot after my father died. I wanted to try to learn from my mistakes. So, I decided to visit Isabella and Alondra, and Chiara's graves. When I buried them, I never thought that I would come back again. But I felt like this was going to be my step in the right direction to heal myself. So, I left them all flowers and I told Isabella that I loved her. I sat and talked with her for a while and even told her how I had fallen in love again. I told her all about Athena and how I treated her. But I was no longer hiding from my feelings and the things that I desired. Athena was happily married and there was nothing that I could do about it now. But I loved her and even though I didn't love her correctly, I'm glad that I let her go. It wasn't meant for me and her to be together, and that's why I did everything that I could to make sure that she found her way back to Satoni. I stood up and started to walk back towards my car. I had sat here long enough and there were still a few things that I wanted to do. As I reached my car I frowned when I saw Aya standing there. I thought that she had left, I didn't understand why she was still here.

"Hey," she smiled.

"What are you doing here?"

She shrugged, "just saying goodbye for the last time. I hope that we never cross paths again. No seriously...I heard about what you did to your father, and I wanted to make sure that you were okay."

I chuckled, "you need to stop worrying about me and worry about yourself. But to answer your question, yes I'm fine."

"What are your plans now?"

"That's none of your business. What are your plans now that you have $1 million and your brother back?"

She shrugged, "go back to college. Pick up where I left off before you came into the picture." She laughed a little, "I'm glad to see that you're finally taking the steps to heal yourself."

"Me too, but don't get your hopes up. I am still Vain Grey."

She smiled and glanced down at her feet. "So, do I see a wedding in your future?"

"I said that I was changing, I didn't say how much. Besides, I'm not a family man, Aya. I'm a man who lives his life to the fullest, and that is what I want to do. Have I learned to value women? Yeah, but I still have the same I don't care attitude."

"So, you're finally going to admit that you love Athena?"

I sighed, she just wanted to hear me say the words. "I love her and that's all there is to it. Now, I'm a very busy man and I have to get going. I hope that we don't cross paths again."

"Trust me, I plan to get as far away from you as I possibly can. But promise me that you will stay out of trouble."

I walked around to the driver seat of my car and climbed in. She stepped aside when she heard my car start. She smiled and waved at me as I started to drive away. I didn't understand her at all. I thought that she would be long gone but she stuck around. It was weird but I knew that she had a good heart. I wished her the best in her life, and I was actually glad that I didn't have sex with her. The last thing that I wanted to do was ruin another woman. I had done enough of that, and now it was time to move on. So, now I was headed to the tattoo shop to add some well needed ink to my body.

The one thing that I wanted to do more than anything when I was a kid was to play basketball. My father always told me that it was a waste of time. He didn't want me focusing on anything that wasn't important to the mafia. I pulled up to the basketball court and was shocked to see Roman playing by himself.

I climbed out of my car and smiled. This reminded me of the old days. I was glad that Roman was here because there was so much that I wanted to talk to him about. It was so much that I needed to apologize for. I walked over to him and he tossed me the ball without saying a word.

"Are you as good as you were when you were six?" I laughed.

He smirked, "I will never lose my touch."

"Well, it seems that I have just been challenged."

"And if I know you as well as I think that I know you, you love a good challenge." He smiled and ran his fingers through his sweaty hair.

Having Roman as an enemy for so long was exhausting. He was humble just like his father. He had his mother's smile, even if he didn't want to admit it. I was happy that we were finally playing basketball again after all these years. I knew that it would take time to build a bond with him because of everything that happened. But I knew the importance of sticking together and treating my brothers the right way. Adonis was right when he said that we may not be related by blood, but we were brothers. We were the four brothers of the mafia and it was crucial that we got along.

"Loser has to buy drinks tonight," I chuckled.

"Deal," he laughed.

The sun was shining bright and after a long game, we were both exhausted. We took cover under a very thick tree that provided really good shade. I was covered in sweat and so was he. The basketball game was fun, but I lost. Roman was right when he said that he hadn't lost his touch. He had gotten better over the years, and it didn't surprise me at all. As we lay there sweaty and trying to catch our breath, I couldn't help but feel like a little boy all over again. I glanced up at the sky, and took a deep breath.

"I'm sorry about my father and what he did to your parents."

Roman cleared his throat and sat up. "Thanks, but it's in the past now. I hate that it happened, but there's no point in getting upset about it anymore. Besides, you evened the score when you killed him."

I sat up slowly and smiled. "I feel the same way. By the way, I lost, so drinks are on me tonight."

Roman laughed, "I'm really looking forward to this." He stood up and offered me his hand which I took and he pulled me to my feet. He glanced at my chest and raised an eyebrow, "is that Athena's initials?"

"Yeah, she means a lot to me. I know that she is with Satoni and I respect it. I mean, everything I did was to better her life. I knew that she would continue to run away from Satoni, so I got her pregnant."

"But you were going to kill the baby. Why?"

"Because I thought that I could fix the mistake I made. I was always torn between keeping her to myself or doing what was right. I'm glad that she found out, and went back to him before I could go through with it. Love makes you do weird shit sometimes. It's bad when you love someone that you aren't supposed to."

"That's true, did you get a chance to talk to her?"

"Yeah, we talked a few days ago. I'm glad that I gave her the closure that she wanted. Now, we can both move on."

He laughed, "you have her initials on your chest. How are you going to move on?"

I smirked, "I can get yours too if you want. I mean I owe you guys so much more than just a tattoo. My family did a lot of damage to yours."

"It's cool, I'm glad we fixed it. We don't want to continue to be like this when we are old. It's good that we are getting along now and repairing our bond with each other. Besides, it wasn't all your fault. You were trying to please your father and I know how that can be. I used to try to please mine all the time, and it was tough. They wanted us to be just like them, and it's funny because we are nothing like them."

"You have a point. I know that I don't want to be anything like my father. So, what are you going to do now? Everything is peaceful between all of us." I was curious to know what he was going to do now.

He shrugged, "my family has a few secrets that I want to uncover. So, I'll be doing a lot of research to try to find out what the Vintalli family was really built off of."

I patted him on the back as we walked towards the car. "Good luck, you're going to need it."

I was learning more and more about myself. I knew who I wanted to be, and it wasn't the man that my father was building. He was treating me like a soldier instead of a son. I was so glad that those days were over. Now, I was headed to the bar to have drinks with Roman. I could learn more about him and hopefully help him with uncovering information about his family. Things were peaceful and I could only hope that they would stay that way.

EPILOGUE

I walked towards the water and I could see Satoni standing there. He told me that he wanted to meet with me before he left Spain. I wasn't sure what he wanted to talk to me about because I thought that we said everything that we wanted to say to each other. But I guess there was something that he wanted to say to me without everyone else around. I stood beside him and stared at the sun setting in the distance. It was beautiful and it had been a while since I noticed just how beautiful it was. The birds were flying in the sky silently and I smiled. This is what peace looked and felt like. Satoni cleared his throat and I looked at him.

"I wanted to meet with you because I wanted to give you two things. They are very important to me and I trust you enough now. Before I get into that though, I feel like I owe you an apology. I took someone away from you that you loved. I could have saved her, but I didn't. I hated you so much that I wanted to see you suffer for what I thought you did to my sister. But now, I see that it was wrong what I did. I have Athena now, and she means the world to me. I couldn't imagine her begging someone not to hurt her, and they do anyway. Isabella was your world and I took her from you. I should have done more. I should have told my father to stop, but I didn't."

"You know the feeling because you lost Alondra." I sighed, looking out at the water.

He nodded his head, "yeah. I didn't want to see her get hurt. I tried to save her, but I couldn't. I cared about her and I felt bad about what happened to her sister. I don't want Athena to suffer because she loves me. I have never loved anyone more than I love her."

"I understand," I whispered.

"Then you know the feeling. I can't be without her...I won't. She is not only my wife, she is my soul mate. She is the mother to my children, and I would kill a million men if they ever tried to take her from me. I feel like because I want to protect her, I hurt her."

I smiled, "I know that you can protect her. You are the leader over all of us, and you're strong. You are the one that we envy. You did what we wish that we could. You got married, started a family, and changed the cycle for all of us. You gave us something to look up to. I have to be honest with you, I'm jealous of and I always have been."

He laughed a little, "I feel like the weight of the world is on my shoulders. I have a family to protect, and sometimes I can't help but think about how easy it was before I got married."

I frowned, was he starting to regret his decision? That would shock me because he loved Athena and he fought to have her. Where was he going with this? "I know what you mean. We only have to worry about watching our backs."

"Now I have to watch my back, my son, Athena, and my unborn child. It's overwhelming. If I couldn't protect Alondra, how can I protect all of them?" He sighed, "this is why I'm telling you what I have done. If I die, I want you to protect Athena. I need you to be there for her even when I can't."

I couldn't believe what I was hearing. He wanted me to step up if he died and play his role in his family. "Why? Why are you choosing me? Athena has Roman."

"But she loves you. As much as I hate it, I know that she loves you. She will learn to trust you, Vain. You have to stop doing stupid shit. I know it sounds crazy, but I trust you with her life. If I tell you to take her and get out of here, do it."

As much as I loved Athena, I couldn't do that to him. I placed my hand on his shoulder. "You are going to be here for a long time. You are going to grow old with her and make five more babies. She is your wife and you don't need my help to protect her. I will be there for her when she needs me. But I will not overstep my boundaries. She is your wife; she belongs to you."

He smiled a little, "thank you. I'm glad that we were able to have this conversation. But there are two things that I want to give you. I want to give you this," he reached into his pocket and pulled out a ring.

My eyes widened; it was Isabella's wedding ring. "I thought that it was lost."

"I held on to it for you. I knew that one day I would be able to give it back. The second thing I want to give you is an invitation to our baby shower. I need you there, brother. You helped protect my child and it means the world to me."

I smiled, "does Athena know I'm coming?"

He laughed, "she told me that I had to invite you. She told me that she would make me sleep on the couch if I didn't." He shrugged and crossed his arms over his chest. "I wanted to invite you though. So, I'm glad that she mentioned it."

"I never thought that we would be like this, it's weird."

"Yeah, after being enemies for years, it's strange. But we will get used to it."
His phone buzzed and he smiled. "I have to get going, Athena needs me.
But you should come over this Saturday, we are playing basketball."

I laughed, "that's sounds like a plan. I hope that you all are ready to lose."

He smirked, "we will see." He turned to walk away, but I stopped him.

"I can't wait to have what you have. You have a place to call home, someone
to go home to. I'm envious of that."

He glanced over his shoulder at me, "you will. Don't envy me, Vain. It's a
lot of work, I'll tell you that. But you will have it one day, you just have to
open your heart a little. You will know her when you see her, trust me."

I watched as he walked towards his car. He climbed in, started it, and took
off. Satoni wasn't a bad person and I respected him a lot. I looked down at
the ring in my hand and smiled. It was nice to have this back after all this
time. I looked up when I heard someone call my name. A girl with short
black hair was jogging towards me. I smiled realizing who it was. I hadn't
seen her in years, and she didn't look any different.

"Savina, what are you doing here?"

She laughed and hugged me, "I was in the area. I haven't seen you in a while.
How are you?"

"I'm good." I smiled eyeing her up and down. The one thing I loved about
being single was doing what I wanted to do. I was going to have fun with
her, just like old times. "You hungry?"

She giggled, "yeah. How about we get some pizza. We can take it back to
my house, and then I'll show you how much I missed you...just like old
times."

I wrapped my arm around her and started to walk, "that sounds like a plan."

One thing I was sure about was that... I was Vain Grey, and I was proud of it.